THE HUNTER'S TALE

Peter Dahl

PROLOGUE

Crosshairs, Far Away

Leif looked through the scope on his rifle and scanned the slope half a mile away for any signs of life. Nothing moved – not even wind through the scrubby grass and the tall pines. It was a still, gray November afternoon, cold and getting colder as the nights lengthened and winter approached. The air was silent, save for intermittent birdsong and Leif's steady, effortless breathing. Nothing from the radio, and it had been hours since he had heard another human voice.

This is how he spent most of his afternoons. Sitting, kneeling, laying, and looking, hour after hour, day after day. Alone, peering through a high-powered scope on a large-caliber rifle, and without interruptions from the extraordinary.

With just a little over an hour left before he would head back in, Leif found his thoughts dwelling on home, thousands of miles away, where he would be doing much the same thing he was now.

He was hungry, and the refrigerator would be full of Thanksgiving leftovers. He'd be home alone, and no one would know if he finished off the pecan pie. After quenching his thirst with a tall glass of water, he'd have a couple of Leinies and fall asleep watching the Bucks game or *The Simpsons*. But first, before any of that, he'd enjoy that feeling of stepping from the bitter cold into the warmth of his home. That was the best feeling. It made the cold worth it. Just thinking about that – about what it's like to be able to finally get warm and dry – could keep him going through those final hours as he would lose feeling in his fingers and toes and those final minutes when breathing became painful and his beard froze.

Leif thought about if he'd rather have a wood-burning furnace and if his mother might still be making pecan pies when a man appeared in his scope. Leif's heart rate spiked for just a moment as a heat wave ran through his body and his grip on the rifle tensed, but he focused on his breathing and settled down as he tracked with the lone figure walking down the slope almost a thousand yards away.

The man was wearing traditional *perahan tunban* linens with a *pakul* cap. He had a prominent beard which looked to be graying, but his easy gait and strong build suggested he wasn't out of middle age.

And there was a rifle slung over his shoulder. Not an AK-47 or RPK, but what looked like a Soviet antique, an obsolete bolt-action rifle. It looked to be part of him, like a tool he always brought when he went out, and like something he wore rather than held with any intent. Even so, this was an Afghani man in supposedly contested territory openly carrying a weapon.

This was what Leif was ordered to watch for. This was who he was allowed to kill.

The man stopped walking and leaned against a pine, like he was resting but moving on soon. He was still alone and his distant, idle gaze was not searching for anyone. He raised a hand to clear sweat from his brow. He must have walked a long way, but he did not appear lost.

Leif's rifle was sighted for this distance and there was no wind. The target was not moving and was facing him directly. A clean kill was all but assured.

Leif didn't shoot. Instead, he thought. Not every man roaming the hills of Afghanistan was an enemy, even if they were armed. He could just be a civilian who carried an old rifle for protection from wolves, bears, and leopards. But he could also be a skilled pathfinder using his knowledge of the terrain to give the enemy an advantage. It was possible he would wander his way back to a camp somewhere and report on the positions of U.S. Marines, or he might hike back to a village where he would eat dinner and sing songs and say prayers with his family.

The shot was his to take. It would be an easy kill and a notch on his belt. If the man was the enemy, job well done. If not, command would justify it and it would be job well done anyway.

But, at this distance, a split second could make just enough of a difference. If the man moved at the very last moment, the kill might not be clean, and he would fall and writhe on the ground as Leif tried to find the coup de grâce.

And, at that moment, the man did move. He resumed his walk down the hill. Leif tracked him, the crosshairs of his scope remaining just above him to account for the bullet drop at this distance. There was still no wind, and Leif's breath and heart rate were steady.

The man climbed onto a large flat rock and stopped again. The scope came to rest, and Leif blocked out everything but the rhythm of his heart and his finger easing onto the trigger.

Whatever else he felt and thought faded away in the severe union of life and death.

One: A Sunday Afternoon

Leif pushed through the Kwik Trip door and stepped inside, holding it for Mrs. Szynski on her way out with a Sun Drop.

"Ope, hey there Leif. Thank you!"

Leif smiled and nodded.

Mrs. Szynski carried on past him and Leif let go of the door.

"Oh, Leif, you seeing your Mom today?"

Leif reached back and caught the door.

"Yup, going over for the game."

"The game's at noon there guy?" she said, still standing just outside the door.

"Just picking up some snacks on my way. I'll make it for kickoff."

Mrs. Szynski opened the Sun Drop on her wedding band and took a long drink. It was plenty warm for early September in Wisconsin.

"Snacks? Mom not makin' a big spread?"

"Oh sure, but I got a special order for the right kind."

"Oh you don't gotta tell me. I always need Doritos for the game."

She took another long drink. Leif waited, thinking she might return to the original question, which he himself had almost forgotten.

"Not any particular kind though," she said.

"Ah?"

"Any kind of Dorito. I'm not fussy."

"Oh, right."

Mrs. Szynski smiled big.

"Well better hurry there guy. Nice seeing you." She turned to go.

"Didn't you want to know if I was going to see my Mom?" said Leif, leaning further out the door.

"Hah! Yeah, almost forgot," she said, turning around and laughing up at the clear sky. "Tell her I can do children's church next week. She asked if we could switch days."

"Oh, will do," said Leif.

"Thanks hon. See yah later!"

"Okay bye now."

The Kwik Trip appeared empty except for Morty, hunched over a crossword puzzle at the counter. The radio was tuned to WIXX, as Wayne Larrivee welcomed the audience back in from a commercial break, probably the last before kickoff.

Leif hurried down the bright, neat aisles to the chips and other snacks. He snatched up a couple of large bags of Combos without slowing and looped back towards the counter, humming the NFL on Fox theme.

Morty looked up as Leif approached and made a shuttering clearance of his throat.

"Leif, how the hell are you," he said, not quite asking a question.

"Yeah, hi there, Morty."

Leif set the Combos down on the counter and reached into his pocket for his wallet.

Morty cleared his throat again.

"Yeah, yeah good. This all then?"

Leif hesitated as his eyes wandered across a box of Snickers on the counter and then the American Spirits in the cabinet behind Morty.

"Ah, no, no that's all just these."

Morty nodded and rang up the total. They finished the transaction and Leif gathered his snacks to go.

"Thanks Leif. Go Pack."

"Yeah, go Pack go."

Leif's parents' house was just a half mile from the Kwik Trip in one of Badger Creek's denser plats. He met no cars or pedestrians after turning off the main business drag. If it cooled down after the game he might go for a walk. He liked the feeling of the empty streets on Sunday afternoons during football season.

There was a fleet of vehicles outside of his parents' house. His old truck would be the last to arrive, and he parked it on the street behind his older brother's new Durango. He got out of the truck and found himself hurrying to the door. It was a few minutes past noon and he wanted to catch kickoff. He also realized how hungry he was and how much he had missed Sunday dinners.

Leif stepped into the house to no acknowledgement. The TV was turned up too loud, and Norris the black lab had died the year before. He left his shoes at the door and headed towards the living room. On his way he passed the kitchen, where his mother, Mary, and his sister, Liz, were making final dinner preparations.

"There's my little boy," said Mary.

"Hi Mom, hi Liz."

"Hey Leif."

"Uncle Leif!"

Leif looked towards the living room to see his nephew Luke running towards him from the living room. He hugged Leif around the waist and then jumped back.

"You got Combos! Grandma never has Combos!"

"I know she doesn't, so I had to fix that." Leif smiled and handed the bags to his nephew.

"Leif, you'll spoil his dinner," said Mary, spotting the exchange from the kitchen. Liz winked at her brother.

"You're right, you might do that," said Liz.

Leif looked down at Luke, who had paused and awaited permission to open a bag.

"Well of course he's going to have his dinner," said Leif. "Especially when Grandma is making – what is Grandma making?"

"Beef roast with mashed potatoes and cheesy noodles," called Mary from the kitchen.

Leif made a sharp inhale. "Oh, that's serious Sunday dinner there, beef roast with mashed potatoes and cheesy noodles. Better save the Combos for a halftime snack buddy."

Luke opened his mouth to protest, but Leif winked at him as he held out a hand for his nephew to give him the bags.

"But," said Leif, loud enough to be heard in the kitchen, and opening one of the bags. "I'm a grown up, and I can eat Combos whenever I want." He nodded to Luke, who grinned and held out his hands cupped together.

"You won't keep that trim figure forever, mister!" said Mary.

Leif poured Combos into Luke's hands and then gestured for him to head back into the living room.

"Oh, well, yah know, good genes I guess."

Leif set the bags on the island of the kitchen and bent to peer in.

"Smells good. Almost ready?"

"Oh yah," said Mary.

"Game start yet?" said Liz.

Leif leaned back out into the hall to listen to the TV, but a collective *YEAH* from his family told him all he needed.

"Yeah must've. I better head in there."

"Ah-buh-buh," said Mary, picking up a serving dish of green beans. "Help me carry these out."

"Ope, of course." Leif reached back into the kitchen and took the dish. "Oh, also, I ran into Mrs. Szynski and she told me to tell you that she can do children's church next week."

"Great! Glad you ran into her. I was starting to get worried she forgot."

"I kinda think she was going to."

Leif took the dish and went to the living room. Typically, Sunday dinner with his parents would either take place around the dining room table or at one of their favorite brunch places, but when the Packers had a noon game the food would be moved out into the living room where everyone could eat and watch the game.

He entered the living room and took a scan of the space before looking for where to set down the beans. His brother, Anders, was on a couch with his wife, Mindy, and their aunt Marge. Mindy was well along in her pregnancy, so soon Luke wouldn't be alone after seven years at the proverbial kids' table. Anders turned to Leif as he entered and nodded with a subdued smile. Leif nodded back. His father, Clint, was in his La-Z-Boy, taking a sip from a Spotted Cow. His uncle Doug was in a smaller chair next to him. And, on the larger couch on the other side of the room, was Liz's husband, Jason, Luke, and Grandpa Delmar, still alive and still awake.

"There's Leif!" said Doug as Leif entered.

"Hey uncle. Food's ready." He gestured with the dish and set the beans next to the cutlery on a low table where the food would be safe. Even when Norris was alive, the food was more threatened by Luke than the black lab, as he had been trained beyond any shade of disobedience as a retriever.

"You weren't in church this morning," said Clint.

"Oh, I…" Leif cast a glance around the room, but everyone was fixed on the TV. Doug was leaning to see around him. His father's expression was as mild as his voice had been. "I guess I just – "

"Dinner is served!"

Mary and Liz walked in from the kitchen bearing the remaining food. Leif glanced back at his father and hesitated, but opted to not finish making an excuse and took a seat on one of the dining room chairs which had been brought out for extra seating.

"Looks good, Mary," said Doug. Others nodded and mm-hmm'd in agreement.

"Well, let's say grace and we'll find out for sure," said Mary. "Who would do the honors?"

"I can," said Mindy.

"Turn the TV down first," said Liz.

Clint pressed the mute button and everyone closed their eyes.

"Lord God, just, just thank you for this day Lord. And Lord, just bless this food Lord and Lord thank you for letting us be together and just, Lord just thank you for being an Awesome God, and, yeah Lord, Amen."

Amen.

As usual, food and conversation took precedence over the game for the first half, but everyone kept half an eye on what was going on, especially when the Packers had the ball. More than once, someone would trail off mid-sentence as Brett Favre dropped back and scanned the field. Clint didn't bring up church again. He could be a blunt man, but he rarely pursued points for the sake of argument.

But church did dominate the conversation, when it strayed away from commenting on the game, as it often did on Sundays. Who was in church, who wasn't, who was getting married or having kids, who was getting divorced, who was out of town, who had gained weight, what the sermon was about, and the like.

Liz brought the subject up when the two of them cleared some dishes and took them to the kitchen.

"Dad was upset you weren't in church again," she said, leaning against the counter with a hand on her hip.

Leif ran some water over a dish and set it in the sink.

"Yeah, I know."

He waited for Liz to go on, but realized she was making him give a reason. "I just didn't feel like going."

"That's not a good enough answer for anyone, especially Dad."

Leif rinsed off his hands and dried them, shrugging and holding back from a full answer.

"I don't know what to tell ya, Liz. I guess I never feel like going. I…I need some time away."

He looked up to see her cross her arms and raise an eyebrow.

"Away from any church? Or just ours?"

"Any church."

Again, Liz waited for him to offer a justification, which annoyed Leif.

"Look, I'm not gonna argue about it with you, and I'll talk to Dad – Mom too – about it sometime. I know that's upsetting to you but church isn't where I want to be right now."

"Well, that's when you most need to go."

Leif rolled his eyes and left the kitchen, grabbing the Combos off the counter on his way. Liz sighed and followed soon after.

Leif set the unopened bag of Combos on the table and handed the open one to Luke, who smiled and reached in for a big handful. Leif paused to watch the TV as the Packers lined up for a third down.

"Leif, move!" said Jason.

"Oh, shit – *shoot* – sorry," said Leif, stepping out of the ring of furniture as Favre dropped back to pass and fired a deep pass. The family held their breath for a moment. The ball landed in Donald Driver's hands and everyone except Grandpa Delmar leapt from their seats with shouts of approval. As the viewers high-fived and toasted and settled back into their seats, Leif knelt beside his grandfather and leaned close.

"Anything I can get for you, Grandpa?"

The old man slowly shook his head. Then he turned towards his grandson and smiled.

"What?" said Leif.

Grandpa Delmar reached his hand over and set it on Leif's.

"I love Sundays," he whispered.

Leif smiled, surprised.

"I do too, Grandpa. I really do."

Leif stood up, then bent down and kissed his grandfather's head. A moment between just the two of them. Then he walked back over to his seat next to his brother, being quick to avoid blocking anyone's view.

After the game, the family lounged around the house for a while longer. Some of them would use the time off on Sunday afternoons to get something done, like water some plants, mow the lawn, or replace a broken window on the shed. But on Packer gamedays, the late afternoon produced a malaise, tinted with either the joy of a big win or a bitter loss, and everyone was just as happy to spend time with family and relax.

Leif, Anders, Jason, and Doug excused themselves to the back porch, where they sipped beers in the shade and talked. Leif didn't understand why the other three seemed so ready to leave their wives inside, but he wondered if it was a married man thing. He didn't see the advantage to men-only, having had enough of that in the Marines, although it did make him feel more comfortable swearing.

There was a collective sigh and lull in the conversation after recapping the game.

"Hey, Leif," said Doug. "I heard your neighbor Betty isn't doing so good. Maybe not long for this world?"

Leif nodded. "That's what I've heard, too. It's been…two months, I think? Since she went into hospice. And it's taken a turn for the worse."

"Oh geez, I didn't know. I had known she was sick but not that she had gone in."

"Yeah, her grandson comes by now and then to cut the grass and stuff like that and he told me it's not long now."

"Couldn't you be doing that?"

Leif took a sip, contemplating whether or not there was an accusation in his uncle's question.

"Sure. And maybe I should. But he's doing it now and knows what she wants done. I think he's handling her affairs anyway."

Doug nodded slowly.

"I mean," added Leif, "I do keep an eye on things, of course. And I've been getting her mail, so."

There was another pause. Everyone took a sip or two.

"This your neighbor whose land you hunt on?" said Jason.

Leif nodded.

"That's good land," said Anders. "Is she selling it, or is her grandson inheriting it?"

"She's selling it. I guess no one in the family is too terribly interested in living there or maintaining it for too long. Seems silly to me, but."

"Maybe you could buy it," said Anders.

Leif let out an abrupt laugh.

"I don't have that kind of money. You know I don't. And what am I going to do with two houses?"

"You could come up with something. Rent it out. It's the fields and the forest which matter, isn't it?"

Leif shook his head.

"I've got enough to worry about."

Anders raised an eyebrow, which he hadn't meant for Leif to see, but he did anyway.

"Oh, well, if it's such a can't-miss, you go ahead and buy it."

Anders smiled and leaned against the porch fence. "Maybe I will."

Another lull.

"Anyway, she's still alive. Maybe Betty doesn't die for years yet. Stranger things have happened," said Leif.

"Could be, but probably not," said Anders.

"Not a bad way to go. Old and of natural causes, ya know?" said Jason.

"I'd love to get to be that old," said Doug. "Though I might have to go easy on the bacon and beer."

They laughed.

"I don't know," said Leif.

The others looked at him, waiting for him to continue.

"Death. It's just so final."

"Is this Intro to Philosophy or…a movie trailer?" said Anders.

Jason laughed. "I can picture it."

"But you know," continued Anders, "I have to say I don't think it's ideal to go that way. If I'm going to face that big dark finality, I'd want it to be suddenly, not a long gradual thing."

"That generally means you don't live as long," said Leif.

"Yeah, would you rather die a clean death when you're 70 or be sick for months when you're 95?" said Jason. "I realize I'm kinda arguing against what I said just a second ago."

Anders hesitated.

"Well, I rather like living. I might really enjoy that extra 25 years. 25 years… that's almost as long as you two have been alive! And you've done a little bit of living in that time."

"You see?" said Leif, cognizant of the dramatic pause he allowed. "The finality of it. It's something to be reckoned with."

The longest pause yet, until Doug laughed.

"Geez, I'm a little too close to 95 – forget 70 – for this talk right now. I got something else for you guys – speaking of hunting. You hear about this deer Lenny Johnson says he's seen?"

Anders snorted.

"Yeah, I heard this nonsense."

"What, what is it?" said Jason.

"Claims he's seen a monster. Big as an elk. Twenty-some-odd points."

"Bullshit," said Leif.

"That's what I said. What most people say."

"See it on his land, or?" said Jason.

"Yeah. Yeah, on his land one evening."

"Ah, the evening – known for its excellent visibility," said Leif.

"Yeah but he's convinced. He's obsessed with it – went out and bought five cameras and put 'em up around the place. Says he's gonna find the thirty-pointer. Or, as he would say it – 'Dah terty-pointer.'"

"Thought you said it was twenty-some-odd points," said Anders.

"Well, you know how these things go. It's a nice round number."

"Lenny Johnson…his land isn't too far from yours, is it, Leif?" said Jason.

Leif nodded, staring off into the trees in the backyard.

"Closer still to Betty's. All the more reason to buy it," said Anders.

"Yeah, I suppose it is," said Leif, deadpan. "But that deer doesn't exist. Well, a deer exists, but not like he's saying."

"Gotta make a guy at least a little curious what he's actually seen, doesn't it?" said Doug.

Leif shrugged.

"Didn't you tell me someone in Afghanistan said they had seen a lion in the mountains?" said Anders.

Leif gave a wry smile, still staring off into the trees, remembering that he had told his brother about that.

"Oh yeah, that's right. A guy did think he spotted a lion. *'A fucking lion. Big as Mu-fucking-fasa'* he said. But lions don't live in Afghanistan. Not anymore."

"Did you ever find out what it might have been?" said Anders.

Leif didn't answer at first. He was still smiling, thinking about the way the Marine had been laughed at for his claim.

"No. We never did find it. Not a bear, not a leopard. Not the goddamn Cheshire Cat."

"So…you never did prove him wrong," said Jason.

"Didn't see a lot of Taliban either, and there were supposed to be a million of them," said Leif.

"Still though. Never proved him wrong."

Leif finished his beer.

"Nope. No I guess we didn't."

Two: The Scientist

"Do you have any sherbet or sorbet? All I see on the menu is custard."

When he wanted to, Leif could analyze and assess a situation with speed and precision. This had made him a decent point guard in high school. He was also capable of slowing down and mulling over the complexities and nuances of a situation, which led him to turn in some praiseworthy English papers when he took the time to invest himself.

In the wintertime, long, free thinking helped to pass the mindless work of snow removal.

In the summertime, his quick thinking – his ability to observe, diagnose, and act – made him a capable waiter at a local cookery, which, along with a winning smile, helped him make an absurd amount of tip money. Leif could maneuver the chaos of a busy dining room with a tray of food while keeping his eyes open for messes, empty glasses, and concerned-looking customers.

However, he was prone to occasional lapses in concentration when his focus would dissipate into rumination, especially on days like this Monday in September, late in the afternoon near the end of a long summer. So, as he filled a diner's water glass, he found himself thinking about the particular shape and composition of the glass rather than listening to the question being asked of him.

"Sir?"

Leif flinched and almost overfilled the glass. He looked over to where the voice had come from. He was serving a table of two older women and their husbands. They were, of course, tourists, and end-of-season tourists who had to make sure everything went right with the end of summer so close. They were probably from Illinois or Florida or both – when he was locked in he might have asked this kind of question, but he had little care for such things at this point in the summer.

"I beg your pardon?" said Leif.

"I said do you have any sherbet or sorbet? I've looked on the menu and all I see is custard. I don't want custard though. It's too caloric."

Leif usually masked his real responses to annoying questions, but he couldn't help a slight hesitation this time.

"N-no. Just custard." Then he brightened his tone. "But trust me: custard is much better. It's worth a few extra calories. And, actually, we have a special where-"

"No forget it," said the woman, waving her hand. "I don't need that. But you really should serve sherbet or sorbet."

"Or gelato!" added the other woman. Their husbands sat mute and dumb.

"G-gelato? Oh, I'm sure that would be tasty. But no, just custard. We're more of a Wisconsin-style restaurant. But there's an Italian place on County L where-"

"No, that's too far and we have a show to get to," said the first woman.

One of the automaton husbands nodded.

"Oh, well – maybe another day," said Leif, forcing a smile.

"No, this is our last day here."

Leif dropped any pretense of friendliness.

"I see. Well, anything else I can get you? The check?"

"I guess that's fine."

One of the husbands opened his mouth to say something – perhaps custard had sounded good to him – but he thought better of it.

Leif nodded and walked away from the table, rolling his eyes and mouthing curses. He locked eyes with Mike, his manager, who smiled and shook his head. Leif grimaced in embarrassment as he approached Mike.

"Go ahead on break after you're done with that table. It's pretty dead right now."

Leif sat in a clean, well-lit corner of the restaurant dining room, sipping coffee and eating a snack of toast with blackberry jam. He was joined by one of the other waiters, a high-schooler named Drew. He was finishing up his break, which he had turned into an early dinner of a pork sandwich and French fries. Leif didn't love working with so many high school and college students during the summer, but Drew was one of those he tolerated well enough. He had been in the same class with his older brother in high school and in college, though they had never been close.

"Tip money good again this summer, Leif?"

Leif nodded. "Always is."

"Yeah, makes waiting worth it. I mean, I like it okay, but sometimes..."

"Oh yeah. I know what you're saying."

Drew took a big bite from his sandwich, more out of hunger than an urgency to get back to work.

"You doing the snow thing again this winter?"

Leif nodded slowly, annoyed behind the masked skepticism in the question. He looked up at Drew chewing his sandwich, and he was disarmed by the sincerity in his eyes. Maybe he was still too young to get the implications of his question.

"Yeah that's not a bad way to make some money either. People are just as happy to get rid of snow in the winter as they are to get lunch in the summer."

Drew dipped a few fries in ranch dressing, unapologetic and indulgent.

"You were the same year as my brother, right?"

"Yes."

"So then what year did you graduate from Lawrence?"

Now Leif was annoyed. Either Drew was pressing on the nature of Leif's employment or he was being oblivious in a way that was not so endearing.

"I didn't. I left after my second year to join the Marines."

"Oh, I didn't realize you served."

"Yep."

"Thank you."

"For?"

"For your service."

"Oh."

Leif took a bite of toast and chewed it with purpose, hoping Drew would head back to work. He didn't. He had seemed to forget about his food for the moment.

"Have you thought about going back?"

"To college or to Afghanistan?"

"To college."

Leif shrugged.

"It would be nice to have the degree. I wouldn't have to wait tables and remove snow."

"What would you rather be doing?"

"Oh, something with the DNR or the parks."

"That's cool. I've actually heard there are a lot of those jobs available right now. You'd be able to get one!"

Leif took a drink of coffee, wondering how much he really wanted to get into explaining his situation.

"I'd need the degree, and I'd need to basically start over. I didn't study environmental science when I was there."

"Oh? What did you study?"

"Political science."

"Well, there's gotta be jobs in that too! Or aren't you interested in that anymore?"

"Not. Not at all. Couldn't be less interested. It was a huge mistake to study it. Well, at the time I liked studying it, but looking back...I just have no interest in that anymore."

Drew nodded, thinking he understood.

"I've thought about studying political science. And joining the military. Like maybe ROTC."

"Oh yeah?"

Someone else might have said *Good for you* or *That's great.* Others more bold might have said *I don't support these wars.* But not Leif.

"Yeah. I'm interested in government. Also law – like law school, ya know? And I've also always sort of had a feeling I should join the military. Since 9/11 at least."

He said it like it wasn't just a few years ago. Like he was an adult, like he was someone personally offended by what had happened. *Damn right, any patriot would,* some people might say. *You don't know what you're talking about,* might others. Not Leif. Leif didn't say anything. Just nodded and sipped his coffee. He realized Drew was waiting for his educated opinion on the boy's future.

"That's sorta the way I felt," he finally said.

He could give his honest opinion – whatever that was. But people weren't always interested in his honest opinion. He could recount his experience. But people weren't always as interested in that – not as interested as they had been before he started the story.

Drew finished his sandwich and Leif took the lull as an opportunity to look out the window at the parking lot. He wished it looked out at trees or water instead.

"You think there will still be at least one war by the time I get through college?"

The question snapped Leif back into focus.

Leif was often asked questions about the military – about his experience or about the institution in general. Many of them annoyed him. Some of them appalled him. He took a beat to steady his rising heart rate. He reached for his default answer.

"Oh at least one. Maybe three."

Drew looked confused for just a moment. Leif met his gaze, dead serious.

"Drew, you're gonna have to order dessert if you spend any longer on this break," said Mike, who had just walked into the dining room. He was smiling, but it carried a light threat. It would be different if it was the middle of July instead of late September.

Drew was startled and turned to the manager.

"Ope, yeah, be right there!"

He wolfed down the rest of his fries, collected dishes and got up from the table, for once not filling the silence with a question. Instead, he nodded to Leif, who half smiled in return.

He took a bite of his toast and chewed it in contemplation as he looked out the window again. Maybe he had been too harsh.

Finishing the toast, he leaned back in his seat and took a few moments to relax, letting the distant buzz from the kitchen and the soft voices of a few diners on the other end of the room settle into a gentle ambience. He sank into the room's warmth which mixed so well with the smell of cinnamon rolls and coffee and homefries. The sun was already getting low in the sky as the equinox approached, casting long shadows through the room. Soon the overhead lights would be turned on and the dining room would morph into dinner mode, but for now it rested in the in-between time.

Leif realized he hadn't checked his phone yet, which was often the first thing he did on break.

He had a new voicemail from Kyle, his neighbor Betty's grandson.

Yeah, hey Leif, it's Kyle. Just wanted you to know that Grandma passed away last night. Funeral will be on Saturday. Well, I'll probably see you before then but I thought I'd call and let you know. We're putting the house up for sale. Should go pretty quick, the market's good. But anyway. Take care, see you.

Leif snapped his flip phone shut. But it seemed irreverent to do it like that. Death was final enough as it was. He opened the phone again and thought a nice thought about his neighbor Betty. Then he eased the phone shut and looked out the window again.

Three: New Neighbor

Kyle was right and the house sold quickly.

The new neighbor, whoever it was, also moved in quickly.

Leif didn't know either of these things, since he had lost all contact with Kyle since Betty's funeral. Kyle rid himself of the house and its affairs and along with it any reason to talk to his grandmother's neighbor.

Leif pulled into his driveway in the late afternoon after work. In the fading light he noticed an old Range Rover parked over in Betty's driveway. Other than that, nothing looked out of place. He parked and turned off the engine and sat for a minute, deciding if he wanted to go over to see who was there. It was, presumably, his new neighbor. But maybe it wasn't, and after a day dealing with customers he was in no rush to have a conversation that didn't feel necessary. Of course, a conversation with his new neighbor *would* be necessary, especially since the next day was the opening day of bow hunting season, and he was keen to get permission to hunt his neighbor's land.

Meeting this neighbor felt like a challenge for Leif. As he continued to sit in his car, trying to decide if he should go in or go over, he felt frustrated and annoyed with this change in his circumstances. He liked having Betty as a neighbor. He didn't know this person, and, in order to be a good neighbor, he was going to have to get to know them. And getting to know people could be exhausting work for Leif, especially after a day of pretending to be friendly.

Leif decided not to take on this new challenge until after he'd had some dinner. Maybe a drink, too, to loosen up. And maybe they – whoever they were, if it was his new neighbor – would be appreciative of waiting until after dinner, too. It was unfair to be annoyed with the new neighbor.

He got out of his truck with a heavy step and then realized that it would be dark after dinner, and maybe meeting a stranger like that wasn't the best. Exasperated, he sighed and thought about it some more, annoyed with himself now that he was making so much out of this.

In his indecision, Leif stood in his driveway and fell into the stillness of the afternoon. His selfish thoughts faded away as he settled into his surroundings. The sun was low in the cloudy sky, and the air was gold and still and warm. It was quiet, too late for the droning insects of the afternoon and too early for crickets. The occasional chirping of a bird was little more than a whisper on the air. He gazed down the county highway extending in the distance to either direction, farmsteads with towering silos just visible a mile away, the field across the road extending into infinity. There were no cars passing by, and he could pretend that the four modern windmills on a distant hill weren't there.

Time wasn't a thing. It ceased to run on. It didn't move. The land could breathe and live and grow without the measurements of hours, days, years. Nothing in the world existed but him and the sky and the fields and it could have been anywhere. And he might have been anyone.

But he wasn't. He could only be exactly himself, and he could be nowhere but there at that time. He didn't know if that was liberating or suffocating.

He breathed deeply. It could be either.

He didn't know how long he'd been standing there when he decided to walk over to Betty's house. But walk over he did, while it was still light and warm and still.

He rang the doorbell and heard it ding. As he did, it occurred to him for the first time that it might not be a single person. Perhaps it was a family. Maybe there would be children. He didn't know why, but in his mind it had always been an older, single person, man or woman. It hadn't occurred to him it could be otherwise.

The door was pulled open and there stood a middle-aged woman. This was what Leif expected. But in his mind the woman was always white. This woman was Asian. Short, wiry, with long dark hair. She wore a Packers t-shirt.

"Hi," she said, with a smile.

"Hi there, I'm Leif. I live next door." He also smiled, put at ease by the woman's demeanor. He extended his hand.

"Oh yes! The man who sold me the house, he told me a little about you. So nice to meet you!" she said, still smiling and taking Leif's hand in a strong grip. Stronger than Leif had anticipated. "My name's Jan."

"Jan, okay, yes, very nice to meet you. You just move in today?"

"Yes. I didn't have much to move – they left a lot of the furniture. The man who sold me the house was so kind – he had a trailer and he drove it down to Green Bay to help me move. I'm working on getting unpacked and settled in right now."

Leif was surprised to hear that. Assuming she meant Kyle, apparently he hadn't just washed his hands of the property. It was strange then that Kyle hadn't mentioned the move to Leif.

"Oh, you're from Green Bay?"

"Yes, all my life."

"Oh, well, welcome to Badger Creek!"

"Thank you, I'm glad to be here. I think it's just what I'm looking for."

There was something in the way she phrased that. Leif noted it, and his pause was long enough for Jan to continue.

"You know what, why don't you come over for dinner tomorrow? If you don't have plans. Then you can tell me all about yourself and this land of Creeks and Badgers."

Leif blinked in surprise. This was aggressive hospitality.

"Oh, I…" Normally Leif would find an excuse to decline spontaneous plans. But he had no excuse, and she was doing much of the heavy lifting in the process of intro-duction. "That would be great. Thank you."

"Okay, great! Maybe come on over around 6?"

"Sure, sounds good to me."

"Good, good."

Jan inhaled like she was about to say goodbye, and Leif realized that he couldn't wait until tomorrow to ask his important question.

"Ope, actually, I almost forgot."

"Yeah?"

"I usually hunt on this land. Betty's land – your land. I had her permission."

"Oh. Not on your land?"

It was a leading question, but honest.

"No, my land is just the soybean field, which someone else farms. It's not good for hunting deer. But your land is this field and all of the woods back there. But you know that."

"Ah, and that's where the deer are?"

"Yes. Or at least that's where it's best to hunt them."

"I see."

She didn't seem quite as friendly as before.

"And, you see, the bow hunting season actually starts tomorrow, and I was hoping I could be out there tomorrow morning before work."

"Bright and early. That's good. That's good."

Leif wasn't sure what she meant was good. He hesitated, not sure if he should put his request into an explicit question. Maybe that's what she was waiting for.

"So I was wondering if I had your permission to hunt your land."

Jan smiled.

"Would you do it even if I said no?"

Leif was taken aback again.

"No. Of, of course not. I would find somewhere else to hunt."

Jan seemed surprised by this answer, but then she nodded slowly.

"I don't see why not. You may. Be safe. And don't be late for dinner."

Leif sat at his small kitchen table eating his dinner of baked whitefish, potatoes, and green beans. Most of Leif's dinners involved some kind of meat that he or a friend had caught or shot. He still bought his chicken at the store, but had considered raising them, mostly for the eggs. The potatoes and beans were from the farmer's market. If possible, Leif liked to buy everything local, until it became an inconvenience.

He put a little more of his aunt Marge's homemade tartar sauce on his plate and mixed it with the fish and the potatoes, which he had already mashed together. He thought about Jan. She seemed nice, like most people say when they meet most people. And she really did. He thought it would be interesting to get to know her. Perhaps she was Hmong – many Hmong people lived in Green Bay. Perhaps there was an interesting story there. Certainly there was. And she seemed like someone who could tell a good story.

She also seemed like someone who might have a secret. This was very much a small town thing to do – to take a passing remark about *what I'm looking for* into a reference to something out of the ordinary, something worth knowing, worth gossiping about. But certainly - single women didn't often move from a place like Green Bay to a place like Badger Creek. Not for the farming, surely.

She had agreed to let him hunt – and on short notice at that. But she hadn't seemed thrilled about it. Maybe she had needed convincing, or maybe she was just testing the waters, seeing what kind of hunter Leif was, making sure he wasn't the kind of man who would ignore her and hunt there anyway, who was just asking out of rote politeness.

If she didn't like hunting, that was fine with Leif. She didn't need to like it so long as she let him use her land, and he wouldn't do anything offensive if he could help it. She couldn't see where he hung up dead deer from her house. Maybe she was offended, maybe not, but they could work things out. Leif always felt he could convince anyone that responsible hunting was okay, so long as they gave him the chance to explain.

He paused with a forkful of fish halfway to his mouth, realizing that the deer he envisioned flitting through the woods had twenty-some odd antler points. Or thirty, being a nice round number.

Four: September Bow Hunt

Leif used the evening to gather his supplies and his thoughts for opening day. Neither task was onerous, but he liked his tasks to have the time to be stress-free. Since it wasn't cold and he wasn't trekking very far, the main equipment to be collected and checked were his bow, arrows, and camouflage garb. His thoughts were not difficult to collect, either. He was relaxed, even though the next morning was for him the most thrilling of all opening hunts.

He sipped a little whiskey neat just to take the edge off, but Leif knew himself, and he knew how to find the thrill in nervous energy without it making him anxious or jittery. Shooting free throws, playing beer pong, and taking his sniper tests had all barely registered on his physiology. He had mastered techniques of focus and breathing and he could divert and concentrate his thoughts to remain level. He used to use cigarettes, too, but not for a long time.

The first day of the bow hunt for whitetail deer hunters in Wisconsin was as good a chance as any to get a trophy buck. They were still adventurous and were not on alert, and their movements could be predicted well enough to set up an ambush and take them before another hunter. Leif was not as concerned with the trophy aspect of hunting as most others, but he couldn't resist letting his mind dwell on the thrill of seeing a monster buck emerge from the trees within range of his arrow. Perhaps Johnson's behemoth was really out there. If it was, this would be the time to take it.

If he had felt rushed or unprepared, then perhaps the nerves of the occasion would get to Leif and rob him of sleep or peace of mind. But while some hunters had elaborate or active traditions for the night before the big day, Leif just gave himself time to relax and breathe.

He had scouted the forest on Betty's property – or Jan's, rather – in the preceding weeks and collected trail cam pictures. There were deer back there, including an eight-point buck he had gotten a great picture of, but it was challenging to track their movements. The woods were thick, and almost more like a swamp during seasons of rain. There were very few clear trails or shooting lanes, and so deer could pass by a stand or a blind well within range and yet go unnoticed. But they were there. They had been for years, and while many had slipped past him, he had harvested at least one each year since coming back from Afghanistan. It was still always a challenge, but the challenge thrilled him. He was confident in the site he had chosen for his tree stand.

After getting everything in order, Leif watched a documentary about elephants on National Geographic and sipped a Summer Shandy. He had some left over and needed to get rid of his summer beers before autumn proper began. It still felt like summer most days. He would just have one and turn in by 9 so that he could wake up at 5:30 feeling rested. Bright and early.

There was something about how Jan had said that, too. *Bright and early*. She had seemed to think that was good. She approved.

Bright and early for the hunt, the hunt on opening day.

6:30. Cool air, colored by the rising sun and refreshed by the light breeze. Songbirds singing and a flock of geese passing overhead. The leaves were turning but the canopy was thick, and the air was dim above the dappled undergrowth and loamy floor. Bats and owls had long returned to their roosts, waiting their turn to resume the hunt. Squirrels – hastening without hurry – scampered across the floor and darted through the branches, sensing a change in the air.

Even as he hoped to see one thing above all else, Leif tried to absorb all of this. He remained alert, scanning the gaps in the trees for a sign of his prey. A sudden movement might catch his eye and his breath for a moment, but these were minor trills in the steady rhythm and melody of a morning in the woods.

These are the untold hours. He had passed so many of them hunting – hunting something or other – here or on the other side of the world. So many hours in nature, on someone else's land in a world he was so very much a part of but so small and integrated into.

So many hours of life in the pursuit of death.

These hours passed, one into another, and the sun climbed in the sky. More squirrels, more birds, more shadows and whispers. More moments of focus and more meanderings of the mind.

And then it was 9:00, and Leif needed to climb down from his tree stand and head back to his house in order to get to work at 10:00. Soon he would have these sorts of mornings untethered from responsibility, but not this one.

He hadn't seen a deer, let alone seen one get close enough, taken a shot, or made a kill. He had heard no grunts and seen no tracks. And yet, as he headed back through the forest, unsuccessful in a sense, he smiled, content. He hadn't made the big opening day kill. But it was hardly a failure.

And still, a massive buck crashed into and out of his contented thoughts, there and gone in the flash of a daydream.

Five: New Neighbor Part II

Leif approached the front door of Jan's house. It was 5:58. Any earlier might have been rude. And when she had said *around 6* he was sure that must mean 6. That was how most people spoke. No need to be so precise. But he wanted to be there at the right time, or what seemed to be the right time, because manners meant something to him. Wisconsin was a friendly place, but manners – or maybe decorum, more rightly – sometimes went by the wayside. Perhaps friendly people had a higher tolerance for inconsiderate dress or arrival times. But a few years of dressing, speaking, being a certain way in the Marines had honed that courtesy into regimented behavior. And so he arrived at 5:58 in a dress shirt and khakis. Maybe it was too much.

He wondered again if he'd overdressed as he rang the doorbell, and he was suddenly transported back to a moment in middle school when he had participated in Youth in Government. He had worn jeans and a t-shirt to an event where all the other kids were dressed up. He had called his mother and begged her to come pick him up because he felt so out of place. And that was the last time he had ever been underdressed.

Jan answered the door. She was wearing jeans and a knitted sweater. Nice enough, but she looked comfortable that way – not just in her clothes but in who she was. Leif wasn't sure how he could know that – maybe it was the big smile as she greeted him.

"Hi, Leif, come on in!"

Leif returned the greeting and stepped through the door.

"Shoes on or shoes off?" he asked.

"Oh, off please! Thank you for asking."

Leif took his shoes off and they headed immediately into the kitchen. Normally he would have brought over a drink, but he wasn't sure yet whether or not that was okay with Jan. In the future he wouldn't come empty-handed.

Perhaps it was strange that he was just walking in the door and he was already thinking of *in the future.*

"Dinner will be ready in just a moment. You can actually have a seat at the table in the dining room. Sorry that it's such an awkwardly big table – like I said the woman who lived here left almost all her furniture."

Leif nodded and headed into the dining room. Whatever Jan was making smelled terrific. He couldn't quite tell what it was – there was an assortment of aromas, and they didn't all fall into a category in the way a particular restaurant or particular ethnicity of food might. But all the individual parts were still working together, even as they each called attention to themselves.

"What would you like to drink? Water, iced tea, milk? I'm sorry I don't drink soda."

"Oh, water's fine, thank you."

Leif took a seat and glanced around his surroundings. The dining room still looked much the same way as it had when Betty lived there. Jan had said she hadn't brought a lot, but maybe she still had things to unpack. It had only been a day. He wondered why Kyle or whoever had decided to leave so many of Betty's possessions there. Maybe it's what she wanted.

Jan started bringing dishes of food out to the table. There was a summer salad, bread baked with cheese and bacon, and a plate of thinly-cased rolls which were unfamiliar to Leif. Jan noticed him eyeing the rolls as she set a glass of water by his plate and a glass of iced tea by hers.

"Ah, gỏi cuốn," she said, taking a seat. "A Vietnamese spring roll – or summer roll – I guess. If it's still summer?"

"Ah," said Leif, nodding like he understood what that meant. He could pick out some of the specific ingredients, like various vegetables and prawns, and it looked good, but he was still unsure of what he was being served. He had never heard of it before.

"It's vegetables, pork, shrimp, and rice noodles wrapped in bánh tráng, which is rice paper. Edible paper," she said with a laugh. "And you can dip it in this sweet chili sauce," she said, gesturing to a small bowl.

"Oh, that sounds very good. And I really mean that – this all looks good."

"Thank you. Everything here is kind of a side dish, but I think it all balances out."

Leif nodded and waited for some signal to begin dishing out food and eating.

"Do you say a prayer before you eat?"

Leif hesitated.

"Y-yes, sometimes." It was true, although he never prayed before meals when he was on his own. The answer felt forced. "Although sometimes not when I'm on my own."

"I don't when I'm alone either," said Jan. "But would you like to say one? I think it feels right to do before eating – with others, anyway."

Leif opened his mouth to offer a reason why she should do it instead, but he shrugged and said okay. They bowed their heads and closed their eyes.

"God, thank you for this meal. Thank you for the hands that prepared it, and bless the food unto our bodies. Amen."

"Unto," said Jan. Where most would repeat *amen* at the end of the prayer, she said *unto*.

Leif looked up in surprise as Jan took the summer salad and used the tongs to serve some onto her plate.

"That's a funny word. Unto. No one says that word unless they are praying. Unto. Oh, please help yourself. Bestow some food unto your plate."

Leif laughed and reached for a piece of bread.

"Yeah, it is. I guess that's where I learned it – praying."

He put one of the summer rolls on his plate.

"So you said this is…oh I can't pronounce it."

"Try," said Jan, smiling.

"I don't even remember what you said, honestly."

"Gỏi cuốn."

"Gỏi cuốn," he said with no confidence.

"Close enough for now."

"This…gỏi cuốn," he said, a little better this time, "is Vietnamese?"

"Yes that's right. And, if you're wondering, which I think you probably are, I am Vietnamese. Or my parents were. I guess you would say I'm American, although I can't speak for you. Maybe you wouldn't say that, not everyone does."

Leif wasn't quite sure what she was saying. He also wasn't aware of the complicated concepts of identity this conversation was already in, although he had some notion some things were not right to ask. He hadn't had many conversations like this.

"I can't say I've ever had Vietnamese food before."

"Oh, then I'm sure you will either love it or hate it. That seems to be the way Americans – white Americans – regard it. It's starting to catch on some places. The foodies are always after pho."

"Pho?"

"Maybe you've heard it pronounced like *foe*?"

"Oh. Yes – yes I think I've heard of that."

Leif took a bite of gỏi cuốn.

"This is good. Like, really, really good."

Jan smiled. "Oh I know it is. I'm glad you think so too."

Having helped themselves to each dish, they took a few moments to eat in silence, but soon conversation resumed. Both appreciated that the other was comfortable eating and speaking, giving appropriate attention both to the food and to the other person.

"Well I guess I'll knock out one of those questions you just have to ask, and have to ask in a certain way: what do ya do, Leif?"

Leif gave a wry smile.

"I assume you mean for work?"

Jan squinted and shrugged.

"That's a fair counter. That's what I think I'm supposed to mean. Let's start there."

"In the summertime I wait tables at the Blue Bird Restaurant. Well, from beginning of May to end of September, actually. Which is when so many people make their money around here."

"Because of the tourism?"

"Because of the tourism."

"And then do you hibernate during the winter?"

"I do snow removal during the winter. I have a buddy who plows and shovels driveways and sidewalks for people. I've done that with him the last few winters."

Jan nodded, waiting to see if Leif would continue or if that was all he wanted to say about his work.

"So that's what you do for work," she said when he didn't say anything else. "Then there must be something else that you really like to *do*."

Leif nodded.

"Yep, yep, you've got it. I don't mind working for the sake of earning a living – and I do – but I definitely value my time away from work. I like to be outdoors, and I especially like hunting and fishing."

"Of course! And how was the hunt this morning?"

Her interest seemed genuine to Leif. He told her about the hunt, and explained how even if he didn't see any deer, he wouldn't say that he *hadn't seen anything*, and even if he didn't make a kill, it was certainly not an unsuccessful hunt. Jan seemed to appreciate this perspective.

"And how about yourself. Did you move up here for work?"

Jan took a thoughtful sip of her tea. It was the first time she had not had a near-instant response to a question.

"No. I'm retired." It was the tersest answer she had given. She realized this and continued in a brighter tone. "I retired early – earlier than I think seems right. But I could. Like you, I didn't much care for my work. I was a consultant for an investment firm. Or, for one firm or another once I started after college."

"But it wasn't your thing?"

"I was good at it, but if you mean did I enjoy it the answer's no. No I didn't."

"Well at least it's done now."

Jan sighed.

"I should have quit sooner. Shouldn't have wasted all that time. Especially when I really knew what the game was. I shouldn't have kept playing. But I didn't know what else to do or where else I could get work. But you're right – at least it's done now and I'm here."

"And why here? Why Badger Creek?"

Jan explained that her family had spent a weekend on vacation in the county and she had found it so beautiful and idyllic that she had set the goal to one day move there. It seemed friendly and peaceful, where she could know the people around her yet have the space to breathe, not that Green Bay was that kind of overcrowded city. Leif knew what she meant. He explained that he also appreciated those things about where they lived, and it was why he had decided to move back there even after spending all his life there.

"Moved back from where?" asked Jan. "From college?"

"No, from the military."

Jan's eyes widened.

"Oh, you served?"

"Yes, four years in the Marine Corps. I enlisted while I was in college."

"Well, to borrow your line," she said, her voice serious, "at least it's done now."

In addition to the many people Leif met who supported the mission of the military with ignorance, so too were there those who criticized the institution with no experience or understanding. But there was something in the way Jan said this, a certain earnestness, which didn't suggest ignorance or spite or a driving ideology. And there was a genuine concern, almost a reverence, which made him think that maybe she really knew something of war. As usual, he deflected.

"I'm glad it's done now, too, but it wasn't like that. I mean, I was deployed, but I missed out on the worst of it. It was mostly boring, actually. Now, my Dad, he really went through it."

"Oh?"

"Yeah…" there was a pause that dragged on, seemingly for ages when it was only a moment. Both knew what he was about to say, and it really shouldn't have been as awkward as Leif felt it was going to be. "He fought in Vietnam."

Jan actually smiled. A sort of grim smile.

"So did my father."

Leif raised his eyebrows.

"Well, how about that? We're turning out to have quite a lot in common. Who knows – maybe our fathers met."

"Oh I don't think so. You see, my father fought for the North."

Leif chewed on a bite of gỏi cuốn.

"Ah. That…yes that makes it unlikely…well, thank God they never met then."

Jan laughed.

"The war was hard on my father, too. And, if half of what he told me is true, I very much believe it was a horror for your father."

Leif nodded and corralled a few stray pieces of the salad. He had expected Jan to be Hmong, and finding out that she wasn't surprised him.

"Leif." Jan's voice broke him out of his thought. "It didn't need to be hell on earth for it to be tough for you, too."

It was like she had reached out and set her hand on his arm. She hadn't, but her voice cast that illusion, an illusion which was more real than most things a person feels on a given day. He looked up and smiled.

"Well," he finally said, "we can speak of lighter things."

"Of course, but we also don't have to. If you want to we can, but sometimes I think people say that because they think they're supposed to."

Leif had never met someone who talked like this.

"I guess you're right. But maybe another time."

"Sure, sure. Tell you what – I'll go get dessert, and you think of a lighter conversation topic," said Jan, standing up from the table. "Coffee?"

"Oh, just a little. Black, please."

Jan cleared their plates and went off into the kitchen.

Leif felt nervous for just a moment. He crinkled up his napkin and moved his glass around on the table. His eyes darted around the room from decoration to furniture to the nuances of the architecture and hardwood floors. Something was different, out of place. Something boiled underneath the delightful dinner and conversation.

And then his racing thoughts halted and he was deep in a memory from years ago, when he was in college, just before making his decision to join the Marines. He was driving back to Lawrence. A distant relative of a family friend at church was with him, a young man Leif did not know who was in his first year at the school. He needed a lift and so he caught a ride with Leif. It was a blizzard. They had considered putting off the trip until Monday when the weather and the roads would be better. Leif had wanted to wait – classes were mattering less and less to him now that his mind was almost made up. But Connor – that was the friend's cousin's name – had wanted to be back, and his parents insisted, and Leif decided he wasn't afraid of a blizzard in his parents' Explorer. So they went. It was bitterly cold, and it took ten minutes at least to clear the ice and snow off the vehicle before leaving, and the doors were frozen shut, and the wind hurt as it continued in unrelenting jets. The drive took twice as long as usual as Leif drove at a crawl through the near white-out conditions, the snow whipping across the windshield and his headlights showing nothing beyond a few feet of them. His knuckles white on the steering wheel, he knew from the moment they turned onto the highway that they had made a mistake.

But still they talked, Leif and Connor. Almost the entire way, even when Leif was holding his breath as a car approached from the other direction and he prayed they wouldn't collide and die, even as every car in the ditch drew their attention away, they talked. At first about school, because they had that in common. And somewhere along the way, as Leif explained to Connor what his experience at Lawrence was like, and what he was getting from school, and what he wanted to *do* with his life, he started going on about joining the military. He explained his reasons for wanting to join and his reasons for wanting to leave. He litigated and apologized and defended and argued all while Connor listened, and asked a question here and made a comment there, but mostly just listened, which was much more than could be said for many people who Leif told about his desire. It was a personal conversation – intensely personal at times. But never, not once, was Leif uncomfortable.

It felt like the most natural thing in the world, talking to a stranger in the middle of a blizzard about his life-altering decision.

"Say when."

Leif snapped back to attention as Jan poured coffee from a carafe into a small cup. It made a comforting sound as it filled close to the brim.

"That's good."

A piece of chocolate cake was already in front of him on a small plate. He had somehow missed her bringing it out. She didn't say anything about it then or as she poured coffee into her own cup and sat back down.

"Jan, did you really take the time to bake a cake today?"

Jan shrugged.

"Well I didn't buy it at the store. Although in a sense I did, since all the ingredients are from the store. What a place, Kwik Trip."

"You didn't have to do all of that just for me."

"It's not just for you – I'm eating it, too."

Leif smiled.

"Retirement brings a lot of time with it. And I'm going to fill that time up. And making food is one of the things I love to do in that pursuit. So really you gave me a nice excuse to be in the kitchen today. Cooking for oneself is well and good, but preparing food for others…that's the best."

Her voice caught just at the end.

"Anyway, this is my mother's recipe. But I can't tell you what the secret ingredient is. You'll know it though, when you taste it."

Leif cut some of the cake with his fork and ate it. He smiled while chewing.

"This, like everything, is wonderful."

Jan began to work on her piece as well.

"And the secret ingredient?"

"It's…well…I don't know. And yet I do know."

Jan smiled.

"I knew you would."

Six: Duck Season with Anders

Two weeks passed and Leif remained without a deer to show for his efforts on Jan's land. One morning a doe had skipped through the trees fifty yards from him, never stopping long enough for Leif to take anything resembling a responsible shot. Leif would never shoot unless he knew he would kill. The hours spent alone in the woods before and after his dwindling shifts at work added up, and though he enjoyed spending time in the cool air and changing leaves, frustration crept in.

However, relief arrived in the form of another opening day – duck season. And while he did most of his deer hunting alone, duck hunting was a family matter for Leif, as he only ever did it with Anders. Together they would drive out to one of Anders' parcels of land that featured a large pond, and together they would set the decoys and take turns working the calls. They had been going together ever since they were old enough, and it was one of the things Leif had missed most while he was in the Marines.

They sat in silence as Anders drove his truck from county road to county road in the dim morning light. Leif was wide awake, but Anders was less of an early riser. That suited Leif. He preferred quiet in the morning anyway. The only sounds were the hum of the truck's first-rate engine and the panting of Moose, Anders' chocolate Lab, in the back seat. At times, Leif felt like he did not contribute enough to the hunt – Anders' truck, Anders' land, Anders' retriever – and he wondered if Anders ever resented this. Leif would be sure to pay for breakfast, as he usually did. It was a nice gesture, though Anders hardly needed any help paying for a meal – or anything else.

Leif did contribute a great amount of skill to the hunt. As usual, he took the lead in setting the decoys in the water, with Anders deferring to his suggestions and making occasional agreements to suggest he knew what they were doing. Moose paced back and forth in the grass with expectation. What Anders might have lacked in knowledge of waterfowl, he made up for in his mastery of canines, and as the brothers settled into the camouflaged blind, a subtle gesture was all it took for Moose to hurry over and sit patiently in position.

Leif was also better with the call, even if he never suggested as much to his older brother, who, as tradition, always began the work of hailing and chattering.

And Leif was the more skilled with a shotgun, too. Experienced shooters at the gun club would watch in awe whenever he shot clay pigeons, powdering them almost the instant they were launched, destroying sets of three with ease. And, that morning, when the first group of mallards came in for landing, his lethality was in full effect, getting off three rounds before his brother had fired two, each shot dropping a duck from the sky and into the pond. A violent, abrupt harvest made by a master of his craft. And while it was exhilarating for Leif, and to anyone who might be watching (as Anders sometimes did), the shooter was well aware of the terrible power he wielded. It was a burden he released in a prolonged exhale as the last duck tumbled from the sky and Anders sent Moose to retrieve.

The morning featured several more of these abrupt fusillades. Duck hunting, unlike deer hunting, allowed for conversation, as ducks are not so wary of noise. Sometimes the brothers would talk, and sometimes they would sit in silence for many minutes. So much could pass between them unsaid, and the things which could not were sometimes challenging to express with words. What would go unspoken was both bridge and chasm.

After the bounteous hunt, the brothers headed in for a late breakfast at the Belgian House, their favorite local diner. It was one of those restaurants that managed to stay busy without ever feeling like it.

They sipped bad coffee as they waited for their food to arrive. They had removed their heavier camouflage gear and rested comfortably in a booth in jeans and hooded sweatshirts. Anders adjusted his knit cap, which he had left on to avoid displaying hat hair.

"I know I already said this, but that was a hell of a hunt," said Anders.

Leif nodded and sipped.

"I think I shot pretty well today, wouldn't you say?" Anders said with a slight smile.

"Yeah, yeah you did. Been practicing?"

Anders shrugged.

"I went out to the range with some buddies just to make sure everything was patterned and to clean the rust off."

"Yourself or the guns?"

"Ha-ha. You know I take care of my things."

"Yeah. I know."

"Of course, I can't go to the range without anyone bringing you up."

Leif looked out the window, not sure how he was supposed to answer that. He demurred with a default answer. "Oh yeah?"

"Don't act surprised. If they're not talking about how this is the year they finally beat you in trap, they're recounting some insane shot you made with your two-seventy, or some grouping with a nine-mil."

"Well good training will do that for a guy."

"You could put that training to good use."

Leif snapped his gaze back to his brother. Anders put up a hand.

"I don't mean it like that."

"Sure, but how *do* you mean it?"

"I..."

Anders was interrupted by an approaching waitress. It was Kelly, who had been waiting tables at the diner for as long as either brother could remember.

"Okay boys. Greek omelet," she said, setting down Anders' food - a large omelet, biscuit, and home fries. He smiled and thanked her. "And a hash brown sandwich." She set a plate down with a glorious monstrosity of bacon, eggs, and cheese sandwiched between two massive layers of fried potatoes in front of Leif. "Enjoy!"

Anders eyed Leif's food.

"What a thing the hash brown sandwich is. You hungry?"

"Very," said Leif.

"Me too. I almost wonder if we should share some pancakes too."

Leif's eyes grew wide and he laughed a grim laugh.

"We probably could…"

"But does that mean we should?"

They both laughed.

"Let's not get ahead of ourselves," said Leif.

"Good call," said Anders.

Leif picked up his fork and knife to begin. Just as Anders was about to suggest they pray, Leif remembered and set them back down. "Would you like to…"

"Yeah," said Anders, closing his eyes and jumping into a brief prayer. "Thank you God for a good hunt, and for this food, and for this time together. And protect our cholesterol through this valley of death. Amen."

Leif smiled as he picked up his fork and knife again. Anders did the same and they began to eat in earnest. Then Leif remembered what they had been talking about. Leif usually let things like this go, but he decided to push his brother on it.

"But what did you mean by that? About putting my training to good use – a bag limit of ducks not enough? Or…"

Anders finished chewing a mouthful and swallowed.

"I mean you are really good at shooting guns – all guns – and you could be a 3-Gun champion."

Leif scoffed.

"No really – you could be. You have that training, but you also have a gift. Even before you joined you had a knack for it."

Leif shook his head.

"I'm not a fan of competitive shooting."

"But you do trap league."

"As a social thing. I can't help that I kick the county's collective ass."

Anders rolled his eyes.

"You could make money doing it."

Now Leif rolled his eyes.

"Sure. Maybe. But that's not what shooting is for."

Each statement they made raised the other's incredulity, as if they were going hand over hand up a walking stick to see who would end up on top.

"So as a matter of principle you won't use your gifts to be a winner and make money? Is that it?"

"Gifts," Leif growled as he turned his attention back to his plate, feeling his blood rise.

"Yeah, gifts."

Anders also turned back to his plate, sensing he had reached a dead end with his brother.

There were a few moments of silence, but the taste of a good breakfast wore away their frostiness.

"Damnit I love this omelet so much," said Anders.

Leif nodded and gathered in a perfect forkful of all the sandwich components.

They continued to eat in silence, slowing their pace just a little to enjoy their breakfast. As the food on their plates dwindled, Anders looked up.

"We're ordering those pancakes, aren't we?"

"Oh yeah," said Leif, almost before his brother finished the question.

They eventually finished their meal, full without feeling sick, ready to head home and clean their shares of the harvested ducks. Leif had no plans for the rest of the day, but Anders was going with Mindy to the mall in Green Bay. They wanted to make sure they had everything they needed (and everything they didn't) for the baby's arrival in a matter of weeks.

Leif reached for the check when Kelly dropped it off.

"Hey, I can get it," said Anders.

Leif raised an eyebrow. "I always get breakfast."

"Well, yeah, exactly. So let me."

"No it's fine. You drove. Moose was a good boy."

"True, but, I mean, you're gonna be without income pretty soon here and I just thought…"

Leif tossed the check back down on the table and stood up. Anders sat back in his seat, surprised by his brother's fierce reaction.

"Oh, okay. I see."

"Leif steady there, I don't mean it like that."

"Of course you don't," said Leif, his monotone still conveying sarcasm.

"I was just trying to be nice."

"Maybe you are, but you can be nice for the wrong reasons."

"I…" Anders trailed off.

There was an awkward moment as Leif debated whether he should just turn and walk out. Anders broke the silence.

"You do what you want. But I didn't mean it like that."

Too prideful to let his brother take the check, Leif snatched it up off the table. "I'll see ya around." He turned and headed for the register.

"Yeah. Yeah, okay."

Leif paid and left, casting a glance over his shoulder at Anders, who was sipping the last drops of lukewarm coffee and had a certain smug look on his face, like he was withholding a secret. Leif ignored it and left. He was in the middle of the parking lot when he realized that they had gone to breakfast in the same vehicle. He turned on his heels and stared back into the diner at Anders.

Though he couldn't hear it, Anders could clearly read his brother's lips.

Fuck you.

Anders smiled and got up to rescue his embarrassed brother. It was sure to be a quiet ride home. But that was nothing new.

Seven: Shelter

The weeks between work arrived for Leif. The Blue Bird went to reduced hours from mid-October to early Spring, making just enough to remain popular with the locals and keep the lights on while the owners left town for the colder months after taking in a haul during tourist season. Leif would go without work until the snows began to fall. And, even then, hours at work were inconsistent.

He didn't mind the time off. Some looked down on him for it, others envied him, but he took it in stride as a time to relax and do a lot of hunting, making sure to keep himself in routines and busy enough to not develop bad habits. He meant to take care of himself. Still, much of his time was spent alone at home.

He was home after running a few errands, watching *Deadliest Catch* on the Discovery Channel and drinking a Leinenkugel's Oktoberfest in the middle of the afternoon. If he was bored, he didn't know it.

The doorbell rang, and it startled him. He set his beer down and went, unhurried, to receive his visitor.

He opened the door to find Jan.

"Oh, hello Jan."

"Hello, Leif. I'm glad you're home. Are you busy?"

She was dressed for work outdoors, in sweats and a fleece, a knit hat, and work gloves.

"No, I'm just, uh, no not busy. What's up?"

"I need a ladder. Do you have one I could borrow? It turns out I don't have one."

"Sure, yeah, I have a ladder you can borrow. I'll meet you in the garage."

Jan went back down the walkway and stood in front of the garage as Leif slipped on some shoes and entered from the inside door. He hit the button and opened the garage door, revealing a large aluminum ladder hanging on the back wall. Jan stepped into the garage when the door was all the way up.

"Here it is," said Leif, walking over and lifting it off its pegs. His truck was in the garage and he had to be careful not to bump into it with the bulky ladder.

"Perfect! Thank you, Leif. And you're not going to ask me what I need it for?"

Leif set the ladder down and crinkled his brow.

"No, I wasn't. I don't think I need to know to give permission."

"Fair, fair. I'm embarrassed to say I need it for clearing out the gutters. I only just realized no one has done it, and seeing as I'm the one who lives there, that someone had better be me, and I better do it pretty soon."

She took a step forward to grab the ladder, which was much larger than her.

"Wait, Jan. Let me do that."

Jan stopped and looked up at him, her eyes narrowing.

"Clean the gutters? Leif, I can do that myself. I'm not that old."

"No no, but, I mean it's no problem if I…"

"Because I'm a woman?"

Leif was taken aback, but Jan was smiling. "Not a good enough reason," she said.

"Of course, but, well, you are…I'm bigger."

"Is that an Asian thing or a woman thing? Or an Asian woman thing?"

She was still smiling, and Leif allowed himself to laugh.

Jan laughed too. "Fine, fine. You can help me. You can climb up there with that big white American male body of yours and throw down a bunch of shit for my little Asian lady body to put in a garbage bag. That sounds about right."

Leif blinked in confusion. "I'm just gonna carry this ladder over to your yard now."

Jan nodded and led the way over.

"I guess you wouldn't ask what someone needs a ladder for, other than to just ask," said Jan.

"What do you mean?" said Leif. He set the ladder down where Jan stopped in her yard.

"Like, what is something nefarious someone could do with a ladder? Now, a shovel, now that you've got to ask about. People are particular about where they cause mischief."

Leif shrugged in agreement. "I suppose you're right. Don't know if I would have asked about that either." He felt a slight gust of wind that chilled him. "Hey, Jan, you know what, I'm going to run back inside and put on some more appropriate gear."

"Smart, smart. I'm going to wait here and think of more things I could borrow from you on a don't ask, don't tell basis."

Leif returned and set to the task. Jan had a few large maple and oak trees near her house, and most of the large orange and yellow leaves had already fallen. There had been some autumn rains, too, and many heavy bundles of leaves had packed together in the gutter. He didn't mind this work, and it made it easier for Jan to collect them when he tossed them down, but he couldn't shake the fear of finding the carcass of some bird or rodent in a handful of detritus. It wouldn't be the first time.

"Leif, I have to ask. Or, I don't *have* to, but," said Jan, stuffing a handful of leaves into the almost full garbage bag.

"I know what you mean," said Leif, starting to pick up on this quirk of hers. "Ask away."

"Did people try to make clever little puns about your name while you were growing up?"

"Did they? They still do."

"What?" Jan looked up with genuine surprise. "And they probably all think they are the first one?"

"Yep," said Leif, tossing down another clump. "Guess it's never been mean though. Well, maybe kids thought they were getting me in elementary school, even middle school, but kids will find anything to make fun of. Whatever they think it means to make fun."

"Most kids will, yes. Not all. But most."

"Yeah. I guess I don't know a lot of kids these days, besides my nephew. It sounds like something he would do just to be funny. He's a good kid."

"How old is he?" Jan took a moment to stretch her back.

"Seven."

"Oh, fun. That's a good age."

"Yeah, yeah it is. What about you, do you…" Leif suddenly realized he might not want to ask this question, but it was too late. "Do you have kids?"

"No."

Jan said nothing more about it, but when Leif stole a glance back down at her she didn't look upset. She spat the word out, but had let it just sit there like a cold fact. Leif climbed down the ladder to move it to a new section of gutter. Jan picked up the bag and dragged it along the ground behind him.

Leif's nose began to run, and he sniffed. He looked up at the graying sky and sighed. He needed to change the subject, and went back to what they had been saying.

"Nothing too bad you can do with a name like Leif. Like…like being named Ruben. Not so bad living with sandwich-related puns." He climbed back up the ladder with care.

"Asians aren't so lucky."

Leif paused, thinking about Jan's name and how someone might make fun of it.

"Wh-what's your last name, Jan?"

"Huang."

"Huang? Jan Huang. What did people do with that?" Leif looked over his shoulder towards Jan. He didn't want to offend, but he wasn't sure what kids would come up with a name like that.

"Oh, certainly my name isn't as unlucky as some. It doesn't sound like a penis or silverware thrown down the stairs – you know, the real classics. But any Asiany name can be said in that goddamn voice people take on. You know the one. My name included." Jan looked down and rocked herself back and forth in an embarrassed way. "Which isn't actually Jan Huang."

Leif wondered if Jan was just short for something, but this seemed more than a trivial nickname.

"Oh? What is it?"

"HOA HUANG!"

Jan scrunched up her eyes and called out her name in the most mocking stereotypical voice she could muster.

It was darkly funny, but Leif didn't laugh. Jan did.

"So, yes, you can see what white boys would do with a name like that. Any pun is a reach, but that name is such a melodic stereotype, what are boys being boys supposed to do?"

She was smiling, but the sarcasm was icy. Leif glanced down at her, but after a moment she resumed smiling and let out a shuddering sigh, like she had just had a bracing drink of coffee.

"Anyway," she said. "We're almost done here, looks like."

"Yes," said Leif. As he turned back to the gutter, he wondered if he should ask more about Jan's chosen alias. Was it just to avoid being made fun of? That didn't seem like Jan to him.

Then Jan's phone rang. She let the bag drop to the ground and removed one of her gloves to retrieve the phone from her fleece pocket. She flipped the phone open, and her face dropped the moment she read the name on the screen. She pressed the button to answer and lifted it to her ear, not bothering to excuse herself from Leif. It was like she forgot he was there.

"Yes…Oh…Doesn't matter to me…It matters to you? …So what…Hold on, that's not…Did I say that? I told you then that I…Would you let me talk? Would you just shut up long enough for me to…"

The conversation continued like this, Jan able to get in few words with whomever she was speaking to. Leif felt awkward leaning against the top of the ladder, a clump of leaves in his hand, wondering if he should climb down and leave the yard for a few minutes. Jan had still not acknowledged him since the phone rang.

"No, you, you listen…for fuck's sake, I…Lắng nghe tôi!…"

Jan unleashed a torrent of angry Vietnamese phrases into the phone. She hardly ever took a breath or a pause, just enough time for the other party to respond. Leif cringed. At this point he felt even more awkward trying to leave, but staying at the top of the ladder as Jan shouted into the phone was excruciating.

Jan's salvos shortened into quick retorts, until finally she snapped the phone shut. As soon as she had, she picked up the bag of leaves by the open end and swung it off the ground, over her head, and crashing back down into the ground. She did this twice more, and Leif winced each time, shocked by her actions and hoping the bag wouldn't break.

She stopped swinging the bag, but continued to hold it, breathless.

Leif stared down at her, waiting for her to say something to him, or to even show she knew he was still there.

She looked up at long last. Her smile was gone.

"We're almost done, right?" she said. Her voice was hoarse.

"Yeah. Just a few more feet."

Jan lugged the bag closer to the ladder and opened it.

Leif resumed working, wanting to ask who it was on the phone, but knowing that was inappropriate.

When he finished, he climbed back down and closed up the ladder as Jan tied up the bag.

"Thank you," she said.

"Of course," he said, nodding.

He hoisted up the ladder, then paused.

"I'll, uh…make like a tree, and *leaf*."

Jan smiled a pained smile.

"And thank you for that, too. You're a good man, Leif." She smiled a little bigger. "Now get the hell out of here."

Leif smiled too, and walked back towards his garage. As he opened the door, he stole a glance back at Jan. She was still rooted to the spot, staring off at nothing in particular.

He didn't want to get into her business, but he couldn't help but wonder, in a horrified but intrigued sort of way, what had made her act in a manner that seemed so out of character.

"Who are you, Hoa?" murmured Leif as he entered the garage and closed the door behind him.

Eight: Proof

In the afternoon of a free day which Leif had to admit was becoming boring, he was glad to get a call from Anders asking if he wanted to go to the bar. They hadn't seen much of each other since Mindy gave birth to a baby girl – Audrey – earlier that month.

Leif had to park down the street as The Inn was busy, even for a Friday. It was already dark and the temperature had dropped. Sometimes Leif would forget that he was cold until the sun went down. But as soon as darkness began to fall, whether he was ice fishing, hunting, or patrolling a remote hillside somewhere in Afghanistan, he felt the chill creep in, and knew that it was only going to get colder. And he knew the cold was unforgiving. As he walked up to the door of The Inn, adorned with some surprisingly kitschy Halloween decorations, he knew this cold was just a feeling – he was in a place outfitted for a temperature hovering just above freezing. And yet, the knowledge and the memory of true cold, of advanced cold, of the cold that kills, lingered in the back of his mind, brought on by the dark and its icy promises.

He stepped into the comforting warmth and looked around for Anders. He wasn't there yet, but a group of people he knew from high school were standing around the bar chatting. He wandered over, and as he approached he caught the eye of one of the women.

"Leif! Look at you! Come on over here."

"Hey, Jackie. Rachel. Fellas." There were nods and handshakes as the group happily greeted him.

"We don't see enough of you. Glad to see you're doing good, let me get you a beer," said Logan, who had put on a lot of weight and an impressive beard since high school.

"Oh, well, thanks man. Miller Lite's good."

Logan smiled and nodded, approving of Leif's choice. He leaned onto the bar and ordered the drink.

"You just come down here by yourself?" asked Rachel.

"Ah, no, I'm meeting Anders here. But you know Anders. He's always late."

"Oh, good, good, I haven't seen him either in a while," said Rachel.

"They just had a baby, didn't they?" asked Jackie.

"Yeah, yeah a girl a few weeks ago," said Leif.

There were smiles and *aww*'s.

Logan handed a pint of beer to Leif, tilting it just enough so a few drops spilled onto Leif's hand.

"Ah geez," said Logan.

"Ope, you're fine," said Leif, even though he was a bit annoyed. He took a long drink and glanced around the room. It was busy and noisy. There were a few groups of younger adults, but at least half of the patrons were in their late forties, fifties, and sixties. He recognized many of them.

"So what's new, Leif? How've you been?" said Chris, one of Leif's basketball teammates from high school.

"I'm good. You know. Not really up to much these days." He took a drink, a little embarrassed by his boring answer, even though everyone smiled and nodded.

He decided to add more detail. "Finally got a deer." He wondered if that was an easy out, too.

"Oh yeah?"

"Yeah, a decent doe."

"Ah too bad. I mean, not bad, but you know."

Leif shrugged. "Sure, I'm hoping to get a buck during gun season, but a good deer is a good deer. Does are hard to kill, too, and they taste just as good."

"Fair, fair. Although I have to admit I'm not a huge fan of venison. Too gamey," said Chris.

"Well if you would do more than just throw it on the grill!" said Jackie.

"Oh yah, some venison stew is the way to go," said Logan.

"I don't *just* grill it. I have it processed as summer sausage too."

"You do that at RJ's?" said Logan.

"Yep."

"Yah that's good sausage. They put all sorts of stuff in that. Takes the gaminess right out."

Leif nodded and sipped.

"There's Anders!"

Everyone turned to the door as Jackie announced the new arrival.

"Hey!" said Anders, his face beaming, though his eyes were tired.

They exchanged greetings and congratulations on the birth of Audrey.

"How's she doing?" said Rachel.

"She's good. She's a beautiful little person. And Mindy is just the most amazing mother."

"That's super, Anders. Let me get you a beer," said Logan.

"Oh, why, thank you. Let me see here." Anders turned to look at the chalkboard with the list of beers. "Hmm, how about the Johnny Blood Red Ale?"

"Ah, fancy, coming right up," said Logan, gaining the bartender's attention.

When Logan returned with the beer, Chris proposed a toast.

"Well, here's to Anders, Mindy, and little Audrey."

They toasted and *here-here'd.*

Then they heard a collective gasp from the other end of the bar. They looked up to see a crowd of people jostling for position to look at something on the bar.

"What's that all about?" said Anders.

"I don't know. They're all crowded around someone. Let's go see," said Jackie.

The group migrated towards the commotion, Leif sauntering behind, not as curious. He couldn't even tell who it was they were crowded around, let around the reason for the hubbub. He had been around chaotic scrambles, and this didn't have the nature of one that would be dramatic or serious. The way people were trying to gain a view reminded him of the way his roommates in college watched a friend beat a high score on Nintendo more than the way a barracks flocked to a fistfight.

As they got closer, he started to be able to pick up individual voices in the din.

"Where was it? Where was it?"

"That's not real. You faked it. That's a decoy you fixed up."

"I ain't never seen such a thing."

"Let me see! Let me see!"

Leif got close enough so that he could tell it was Lenny Johnson everyone was crowded around. Some of the older farmers and contractors were closest to him. He was holding a piece of paper, clutching it with both hands, trying to show it around, but fighting off people who tried to snatch it from him. He looked like he was breathing heavily, and he wasn't saying a word.

Now Leif was interested.

"What is it?" said Leif to Chris, who was closer to the middle of the pack.

Joe Mattingly, a commercial fisherman, whipped his head around. His eyes were alight.

"It's the thirty-pointer!"

Leif's eyes widened.

"He's got a picture of it?"

"Yah, from his trail cam! From this morning!"

Leif began to push his way forward, but there was no way to get close enough. He stepped back and decided to wait for people to clear out. His mind began to race. He wanted to believe that such a beast existed, and one so close to his own hunting grounds. But it didn't seem possible. Yet if this was a clear picture it was proof. Pictures could be doctored – he knew that – but Lenny didn't know how to do that. No way.

His patience was finally rewarded as people began to back away, shaking their heads in disbelief and wishing for Lenny's luck. Leif filled the void and looked over Lenny's shoulder at the large printout plastered to the bar by Lenny's rugged, dirty hands.

The picture was almost as perfect as its subject. There was no doubt of what it was, and what it displayed was a deer unlike any Leif had seen. Easily thirty points, and not in the crooked, gnarled, irregular branches and tines which some deer of impressive antlers developed, but in a broad, tall, symmetrical pair of glorious horns, like the symbol of a great medieval house. The animal was huge, and nearby trees gave some context to judge its size. It must have weighed well over 250 pounds, perhaps even 300. The camera had not caught the creature skulking around the woods, but rather had captured it in what looked like a confident – resplendent – pose.

Leif had nothing to say. It was more than he could comprehend. The deer was real. And it was close.

"Never doubted you for a second, Lenny," said Logan, slapping the middle aged man on the shoulder. He was silent for a few moments more. When he spoke, it was slow, measured, and hoarse.

"They said I was lyin'. Said there was no way. And now. And now. Now they know. Now they know."

"Hell yeah they know," said Logan.

"Now it's all about who sees it next," said Chris.

Lenny slowly turned his head towards Chris, taking his eyes off the picture and fixing the young man with an icy stare.

"Oh yah? It's gonna be me. No one else. Put…that…down," he said, tapping the bar with each word, "I'm gonna shoot that deer. It's *mine*."

Chris' face dropped and he hesitated, but Logan stepped in.

"Ah don't worry, Lenny. We know it's your deer. Better hope the deer feels the same way. Keep setting those bait piles!"

Lenny didn't say anything. He just glared for a moment more, and then turned back to the picture.

Leif's brow furrowed. That – what Lenny just did and said – bothered him. He took a big drink and his pint was almost empty.

Chris and Logan turned away from Lenny and exchanged *oh shit* expressions with Rachel and Jackie, and they all giggled as they walked away.

"God, here I thought we were just out getting a couple-two-tree brewskies and Chris is getting a death threat," said Logan.

"That was weird," said Jackie. "He was almost like that guy in *No Country for Old Men*."

"What's that?" said Logan.

"You know, the movie?"

"Oh, haven't heard of it." Logan shrugged. "Is it good?"

"I haven't seen it. It hasn't been in theaters yet."

"Then how do you know what it is?"

"There's commercials on TV, dummy."

Logan shrugged again. Jackie rolled her eyes.

"Honestly."

"Well, anyway," said Rachel, "that was weird. But, I mean, you see the crowd of people? He's not the only one all riled up about this."

"Yeah, Leif, I'd expect you to be hyperventilating with that deer so close to your land," said Anders.

Leif didn't respond. He was staring at Lenny as Lenny stared at the photo, both of them tuned out.

"Leif?"

Leif snapped back into focus.

"Oh, uh, yeah. Yeah that's kind of amazing news. I'll be looking for it, even if Lenny thinks it's his."

"Yikes, you're going all old man in the country or whatever, too," said Logan.

Leif stared at Logan with a mocking, vacant look, and then smiled.

"You live under a rock." He took a drink, but realized his glass was empty. "And I'm out."

"Good thing we're at a bar then," said Anders.

Leif glanced over at Lenny one more time, and then smiled at his brother.

"Yeah. Good thing."

Nine: Phone Calls

October turned into November, with Thanksgiving and the gun deer hunt on the horizon and still no snow to remove. Late one Saturday evening, Leif lay on his couch, flipping through channels, dissatisfied with the evening's selections. *Saturday Night Live* would start soon, but he wasn't sure if he was in the mood for laughs.

He was tired. Drained. Ever since Lenny's reveal, he had been making a point to be in the woods with an arrow nocked by the time it was light out. He was sure others, Lenny included, would be up even earlier. Perhaps a beast like this couldn't be taken during the bow season – maybe it would never walk that close to a human. Maybe an arrow would bounce off its hide like a plastic straw's wrapper. Leif wasn't obsessed with trophies, but this was different. This was less than once-in-a-lifetime, and it had happened to materialize so close to him.

These early mornings followed by an empty schedule which often ended at the bar or on the couch late into the night were adding up and taking a toll. He had tried to maintain his track record of eating well, staying busy, and getting exercise, but too often he came back from the woods for lunch and felt like doing little more than lying around the house. Reading and cooking sometimes seemed too much compared to watching TV or playing Xbox.

On this night he went with Chinese takeout after a day of playing *Halo*. It was getting colder, and he had warmed up with an entire pot of coffee, and to calm down he started drinking earlier than normal. Not to excess, but enough to counter (at least in his mind) the caffeine jitters.

He surfed his way to the BBC and was met with a headline about the bombing of a factory in Baghlan. Dozens dead.

"Christ."

He continued to surf.

He didn't used to get so tired like this. He played sports in high school, studied hard in college, done a tour in Afghanistan, and completely renovated this disaster of a house he had bought. He never felt so weary. Now, days of sitting were wearing him down, and that didn't make it any easier to get back into good habits.

The only time of day when he felt fresh and fully himself was first thing in the morning as he stepped out his back door and began the hike across the soybean field to the forest. The crisp air filled his lungs, cleared his mind, and energized his body. He was awake and alive and invested in the moment and the steady unfolding of a day in the numinous woods, where, somewhere, a beast out of legend was walking. He felt fully the huntsman, now being pushed to the limits of his skill to do what few people – ever – had done in taking such a prize, a prize which could not be encapsulated by a head on a wall or a feature in *Field and Stream*.

But Leif would not wake up early the next morning. If there was ever a day to sleep in, it was Sunday. Roll out of bed, have a late breakfast, sit around and watch football, maybe go for a walk for some fresh air after that, order a pizza and watch more football. That seemed good to him as he flipped from a Robert De Niro film he couldn't remember the name of to *The Simpsons*, which he almost always stopped on. He was just too tired to get up early for a hunt yet again, and he could go in the afternoon if he felt like it.

The family hadn't gathered for a Packer game since Audrey was born and Grandpa Delmar caught a scary cold. There were hopes they would still all get together for Thanksgiving, which the Packers happened to be playing on. Leif loved Thanksgiving gatherings, but he loved it so much more when everyone could be there and be well. But he would spend tomorrow alone, trying to relax within the mire of uncontended solitude.

Leif woke up on the couch to the sound of a generic ringtone. He took a moment to process where he was and what time it must be. He hadn't meant to fall asleep, and he had no idea how long he'd dozed. The TV was still on.

He reached over onto the end table and grabbed his cell phone. The small screen on the outside said it was 7:27 a.m. He'd slept straight through the night.

He flipped open the phone to see that his father was calling. He sighed a heavy morning sigh and pressed the green button.

"Hello?"

"Leif. It's your father."

"Yeah, I know."

"Are you coming to church today?"

"Wha- I…" Leif paused for a beat. Why was he asking this? "No. I'm not."

"Why not? You should."

His father's tone was gruff and matter of fact. But not quite angry.

"I don't know. I don't really go anymore. You know that."

Now his father paused.

"I know. And that's disappointing."

"Sorry to disappoint you," said Leif, shaking his head, confused and a little annoyed.

"No, no, I don't mean it like that. Not like you're not living up to my standards. I just think it would be better if you went. It would be good for you."

Leif's gaze wandered over to the empty cartons of Chinese on the table. He looked at the TV and realized it was *Good Day Wisconsin*. Maybe this wasn't the best way to begin a Sunday. He felt slight private embarrassment, but he had no desire to go to church.

"N-no. Thanks for asking." He yawned.

"Did I wake you?" said his father, still gruff.

"Yeah, you did, actually."

"Not like you to be sleeping in so late."

"It's not. I'm always up by now. I just…felt like sleeping in today."

Another pause.

"Next week then."

"Uh, maybe. We'll see."

It was a rote response. He had no intention of going.

"Okay. Well, uh…you'll be over for Thanksgiving, right?"

"Yeah, I wouldn't miss it."

"Well that's good then."

"Yeah."

"Okay. Well, hopefully I see you before then."

"Maybe."

"Gotta go now. Bye, Leif."

"Bye, Dad."

Leif closed his phone and slumped back down into the couch. The call had woken him up, but he still felt foggy. He would have settled right into a comfortable position and let himself sleep a couple more hours if not for the need to piss.

After using the bathroom, Leif went to his back sliding door and slipped on some shoes. If he was going to be awake, he might as well try to feel present.

He slid open the door and stepped into the crisp morning air. As usual, a deep breath made him feel alive and free and at ease with his place in the world. He stretched his arms and back and looked out across the soybean field. There happened to be a lone deer wandering across it about 200 yards away. His attention laser-focused for a brief moment, but he could tell it was a doe. He scanned the edge of the field to see if there were others but the deer remained alone. He smiled. He was no danger to the deer right now. Under the circumstances, the deer was actually the greater threat, part of a huge population of crop-destroying, car-crashing pests. It wasn't their fault. They were just being deer. There were just too many of them because there were too few wolves.

Or maybe just too many people.

They were beautiful, too, even if they were pests.

And tasty.

Leif felt hungry. With a sigh, he went back into the house and opened the fridge to begin preparing himself some breakfast.

A phone call woke Leif up the next morning, too. The TV was on again, just returning from commercial break to *Good Day Wisconsin*. Leif blinked and stared at the ceiling, not sure for just a moment if it was actually Monday. He reached over for his phone, not expecting it to be anything too urgent, but he snapped wide awake and sat up straight when he read the name on the screen.

Bryan Foley.

He rushed to answer.

"Hey it's Leif."

"Jensen! Hey, it's Foley."

Foley had a high, nasal voice, and there was a quiver even in his cheerful greeting.

"How are you, Foley?"

"Oh, not too bad. How about you?"

"Yeah I'm good. Doing good."

"That's good."

There was a long pause and Leif's heart raced. He had an idea of what was about to happen.

"Actually I'm not so good," said Foley. "It's...um..."

"Go ahead."

"It's the V.A. I'm just...I'm having trouble with them again, you know? I need to go in, but...ah...ah fuck, Jensen..."

"It's okay, Foley."

"I get confused and I can't keep track of everything and I...you know how it is. It's a big clusterfuck and I just...."

"I know, I know. It's okay. You want me to go in with you?"

"Would you? I don't want to impose."

"It's no problem. When did you want to go?"

"Could...could we go today?"

Leif put his hand over the phone and sighed.

"Yeah. Yeah we can do that. I can be there sometime in the middle of the afternoon, if that's okay."

"It'd be great. Yeah, that's perfect."

Leif could hear the relief in Foley's voice.

"Okay. I'll call you when I'm getting close."

"Thanks Jensen. Thanks so much. I'll see you soon."

"Yep. See you soon."

Leif ended the call but did not close his phone. He let his hand rest on his knee and stared idly at the TV for a few moments, not hearing what the hosts were saying, instead hearing Foley's high voice belting out marching cadences alongside him on a muggy day in Paris Island. Then he heard the thrum of a transport helicopter in Bagram and he could see Foley smiling at him as the two parted ways, Foley's shoulders rolling in a light swagger. And then he was in the middle of a dim office, a flickering fluorescent light illuming Foley's sunken features as he moved with a slight limp on a carbon fiber leg.

He turned his attention back to his phone and called Anders. He started to get nervous as the ringer continued.

"Leif?"

"Yeah, hey Anders. Are you at work yet? Do you have a sec?"

"I just got in but yeah I've got a minute, what's up?"

"I...uh...Foley called."

"Oh. Is he okay?"

"No. I mean he's not hurt but he's having trouble with the V.A. again. I'm going down to Green Bay to help him again."

"Oh good, good."

There was a long silence.

"I..." began Leif.

"So yeah do you...uh..."

"I mean it's not, you know."

"No I know. What...what time?"

"Middle of the afternoon? Can you get off by then?"

"Yeah, but why rush? Let's go now and we can get lunch after and I'll be home early to help with Audrey."

"Oh, oh okay. That'd be great. I'll call him and make sure that's fine."

"Good. I'll leave now. Be there before you're out of the shower."

"Okay. See you soon."

Leif blinked away a tear as he hung up and went to dial Foley's number. He had cried the first time he had made that call to Anders, trying to explain why it was so hard for him to go help Foley even when he was more than willing to do it. Now he teared up because his brother didn't make him explain anything.

Ten: Through the Door

"It's great you do this."

Leif jumped at the sound of his brother's voice. He had almost fallen asleep looking out the window as they drove in silence along Green Bay (the body of water) towards Green Bay (the city).

"Did I wake you?"

Leif shook his head and grunted.

"I was just saying I think it's great you do this. Really, I do."

Leif shrugged.

"He was one of my best buddies."

That was all the explanation Leif gave, even though there was more to say. Foley was a Marine Corps sniper, too, and their deployments in Afghanistan were interchangeable. It could just as easily have been Leif in that Humvee. But his brother knew that.

"I know. I just know you wouldn't ask me to come....you know."

"I know."

Anders' truck sped along, and Leif felt himself getting drowsy again, even though they were getting close. He might have fallen asleep if he hadn't asked about Audrey, and every answer Anders gave was steeped in new father pride.

Anders dropped Leif off at the V.A. before going to pick up some things at Menard's. The office was in the basement of a plain concrete and brick building on the outside of a business district. Leif saw a blue pickup truck in a handicapped spot and thought he recognized it as Foley's. He took a deep breath and headed in, not needing to check the directory for the office.

Before pushing open the heavy wooden door into the basement office, Leif looked through the glass wall and saw Foley sitting in a chair. Leif's breath caught, and his hand froze on the doorknob. Even dressed for the weather, Foley looked thin and his face was pale and gaunt. His eyes were sunken and shadowed, and his hair was matted. He had been wiry and strong before, and had bright eyes and a quick smile. Now he was staring at a clipboard in his lap, not making any effort to fill it out, looking defeated by yet another stack of papers.

Leif pushed the door open, waiting for the moment when Foley would look up at him, dreading what he might see as much as what he might not find there anymore.

Anders picked up Leif an hour and a half later. He started driving towards downtown where they would decide where they wanted to get lunch.

"How was that?"

Leif shook his head.

"He wants more drugs and they don't want to give them to him. The counselor he's been seeing won't recommend a different drug and so he wants to get set up with someone else but they're slow in doing that. According to our calculations, they're behind on his disability payments, but according to their records they've sent him one check too many. It's just...it's fucked."

Anders didn't respond.

"He's addicted to those pills. He wants more and different kinds and...I know he's in pain but it can't be good to just keep taking them like this. It's just..."

"It's fucked."

"Yeah. And I wish I could help him more. I think we might've done enough for him to get to see a new counselor - he's supposed to call back next week for an appointment. And I hope that helps. And apparently there's some other vets who are organizing to file complaints or something. So. Guess we'll see."

He let out an exasperated sigh.

"Well, just being there had to mean a lot to him."

Leif shrugged again. "I hope so. He needs it."

"I know you did what you could. Let's get lunch now, yeah? You look like you need it."

Shaken as he was, Leif admitted to himself food sounded good.

"Where do you want to go?" said Anders. "What do you feel like? Burgers?"

They were not quite to the part of town where they would start to find more restaurants.

A weatherworn sign and a blinking neon bowl with the word 'Pho' caught Leif's eye.

"Let's go there."

"Where?"

"There," said Leif, pointing.

"What is this place?" said Anders, slowing down and putting on his blinker, still not sure where he was pulling into.

"Uh, Number One Noodle House, I guess," said Leif.

"Do you know this place?"

"No. But they have pho and I want to try it."

"Pho?" said Anders, parking the car but not yet cutting the engine. "What is pho?"

"You might have heard it mispronounced as 'foe.' It's a Vietnamese soup."

"Ohhh. Yeah. I think I've heard of that. Did Jan tell you about it?"

"She did, yeah."

"And you want to try it...here?" said Anders, eyeing the restaurant.

"Yeah sure, why not?" he looked over at Anders, who gave him an incredulous side-eye. "Rhetorical question," he added. "Come on, let's go."

Leif started to get out of the car as an old Range Rover came around the other side of the restaurant and made the turn out onto the main road.

"Is that..." Leif thought he recognized the car, and then he caught a brief glimpse of the driver, who looked familiar too.

"I think that was Jan!" said Leif, turning to Anders.

"Really?"

"Yeah, I..." he thought he recognized her license plate, too, but he second-guessed himself. "I think it was. Well, that's an endorsement for the place. Come on."

Leif led the way into the restaurant, looking forward to trying pho but also thinking about the possibility that someone here might know his neighbor. Of course she didn't know every Vietnamese person in Green Bay, but he thought there had to be some chance.

There were not many tables inside, but there was at least one person seated at every one of them. There was a register at the counter underneath a hand-written menu. A younger-looking Vietnamese woman stood behind it.

"Well it smells good," said Anders as they headed towards the register.

The woman greeted them.

"Hi, did you know that woman who just left?"

Leif blurted the question before thinking. He was surprised by how interested he was in knowing anything related to his new neighbor.

The woman didn't mask her surprise and confusion. "The little Vietnamese woman who just left?"

"Yes," said Leif, his voice excited, as if she had done more than just respond to his question.

"I know her. Do...do you know her?"

"Yeah, her name's Jan. Or...Hoa."

The woman looked surprised again, but not confused.

"Oh you do know her then. Yeah, Hoa's my cousin. I'm Minh."

"Nice to meet you," said Leif, beaming. "This is my brother, Anders. Jan's my neighbor."

Minh looked a little concerned by this revelation. "In Badger Creek?"

"Right."

The woman nodded. "*How* well do you know her?"

Leif hesitated. "Um, just a little."

Minh continued to nod. "Get to know her a little better, would you? I don't know if she knows what she's doing."

Leif blinked. "What she's doing?"

Minh shook her head. "I'd like to take your order now, if that's okay?"

Leif hesitated again, feeling like he was being shut out at a crucial moment. "Oh. Um, of course. I…" he looked up at the menu, forgetting what had brought him in the door in the first place.

"We want pho," said Anders, stepping up next to his brother and pronouncing the word correctly. "Two bowls of beef pho and two orders of pork egg rolls."

Minh smiled as if nothing was unusual about their interaction. "Coming right up," she said, punching buttons on the register.

Pho and egg rolls sounded good to Leif, but as Anders procured his wallet and Minh called back into the kitchen in Vietnamese, he realized that wasn't, after all, what had really brought him in the door.

Eleven: Night, Gun Hunt

It was the evening before Badger Creek's most anticipated gun hunt in living memory.

Lenny's deer, which had taken the inevitable moniker of The Thirty-Pointer, was common knowledge in the area. An unwritten code compelled citizens to hide its existence from outsiders. Some blabbed, of course, but without a copy of the picture, no one was going to believe them. But local hunters young and old knew that it was real, and with the range afforded by a high-powered rifle, everyone believed that they had a chance if they could just get one glimpse of the beast. Many laid out bait, hoping against hope that the wily creature would be so foolish. The weeks leading up to the hunt had been busy times at the gun ranges, with rifles sighted in and targets set well beyond distances of certainty.

All this was in addition to the usual anticipation of this day, a day which was already one of the most anticipated of the year.

Leif couldn't sleep.

He was not his calm self. Try as he might to stick to his principles and to tame his imagination, this monster deer was the one thing on which he fixated in his largely unoccupied time. Every hunt mattered to Leif. Every game sighting was a thrill, every shot a holy ritual, every kill a sacred act, every cleaned, prepared, and cooked animal a profound rite and entry into life's coursing. But this creature, this one-in-a-million creature, seemed so much more meaningful. Leif thought of every animal as a small miracle in a natural world of miracles, but this one was more special, if not innately, then because people had decided so.

He deliberated where he should set up to give himself the best chance. In the woods, the deer had the advantage of remaining unseen until it was close enough to sense a hunter. Across the field, the deer might emerge from the woods just a step where it felt it was safe, and Leif's great advantage of a powerful rifle could be employed even at that great range. It was a long shot, but one Leif was almost sure to make. It was not a guaranteed clean kill, but perhaps it gave him a better chance of having an opportunity to even take a shot.

There was a part of Leif that wanted the deer to go on living forever, existing like a phantom seen only in fleeting moments. But with so many guns in the woods, it seemed impossible that it could survive much longer, and if someone was going to take it, he wouldn't mind if he were the one to do it.

Interspersed in his various thoughts about the hunt and the deer, Leif would suddenly encounter some other nagging thought, something else that bothered him. Images of financial spreadsheets, of family gatherings, of church pews, of somber barracks, of a snowy campus, of people he used to know - these would flit in and out of his thoughts and catalyze a second-guessing of his decision to hunt in one place or another, or would make all the more vivid his dream of seeing the deer emerge from the trees and settle into his crosshairs.

Unable to settle down enough to lie down and try to sleep, he decided to take a walk outside. It was very cold, but if he put on a few layers. The fresh air would do him some good.

The air took his breath away when he stepped outside, but this feeling was soon replaced by an invigorating freshness. He stepped out into his backyard and began walking out towards the woods with no real destination in mind. About halfway across the field, he stopped in his tracks and became gripped with the thought that he might leave too much scent and scare away any deer that might come through in the morning. He turned back and quickened his pace away from the trees. He decided he would walk along the county highway for a little ways instead. There wouldn't be many cars, but if he saw headlights he would step down into the ditch until they passed. He knew he was invisible to them until it was just about too late.

It was cold, being close to midnight in mid-November, but Leif didn't mind, so long as he was walking and knew where he was and where he was going. He wouldn't do anything foolish to challenge the cold's power.

He was reminded of night patrols in Afghanistan. He had often enjoyed these. There was – in theory – the potential for an ambush, but it never happened, and eventually these patrols felt more like PT than combat operations. It was cold – sometimes unbearably – but it was a sort of comfortable robustness, a challenge that helped him feel alive as he trudged through the hills and forests with his comrades, keeping an eye out for danger but breathing easy all the while. Time breeds invincibility. And he spent plenty of time on patrol.

After going about a half mile down the road, Leif turned back towards home.

As he approached his driveway, he could feel tension in his chest and random anxious thoughts pinging around in him, and despite the cold he was not ready to go back inside and get ready for bed. Outdoors felt safer. He wandered into his backyard, still with no intent or objective.

He looked over towards Jan's backyard. He had never seen it, let alone been in it, since she had gotten settled in. It was surrounded by a perimeter of thick hemlock making a natural privacy fence, insofar as intentionally planted trees can be considered natural. Leif was not one to trespass, but his listless night wandering engendered apathy for decorum. And, while the last time he had spoken to Jan ended in bizarre fashion, he felt they had a good enough relationship where she would understand – or at least not be upset – if she happened to be up looking out her window at midnight and found him having a look about.

He pushed his way through the hemlock branches, careful to keep them out of his face in the darkness. There may have been enough space for him to crouch and shuffle under them, but bundled up as he was, pushing through seemed easier.

When he emerged from the trees, he was surprised to find that most of the lawn had been churned up and that extensive landscaping had been done since Betty had lived there. In the visibility provided by a half-moon on a clear night, he could see that rows for planting had been prepared, a box garden installed, and contours and elevations fashioned. There were some open spaces which looked like they might be spots for planting trees. It was not a particularly large yard, and it appeared Jan was using about every inch of it to grow something. She must have been busy through the last two months making these preparations so she could begin to plant in the spring.

"Hello, Leif."

His heart jumped in his chest and he spun around towards the house. Jan was sitting on the steps leading up to the deck.

"God, Jan, sorry, didn't see you there, and, um, sorry for being in your yard without…"

"It's fine, it's fine," said Jan. There was warmth in her voice which Leif could detect even with her sitting twenty feet from him and obscured in the dark. "Come on over, have a seat."

"Oh, I…" Leif hesitated and was unsure why.

"You must. This is a citizen's arrest. Trespassing. Conspiracy to burgle. Now I must question the burglar."

Leif smiled and sauntered over to her and sat down beside her on the steps.

"It's late and cold to be out and about," said Jan, her chin buried in the shoulder of her jacket as she looked over and up at him.

"I could say the same to you."

"Yes. You could. And you have. Did you not find what you were looking for in your yard?"

"No, I didn't. In more ways than one."

"Oh, and were either of your searches fulfilled in my yard?"

"I suppose that remains to be seen."

"Leif, are you flirting with me?"

Leif's eyes widened. "What? N-no, did I make it sound like that's what I was saying?"

Jan dissolved into mirthful laughter. She slapped him on the leg and came down from her laughter with a sigh. "That was mean of me. No. No you didn't. I'm kidding. And anyway, I'm gay."

Leif's eyes narrowed this time. He hesitated too long to respond, and Jan guffawed again. She slapped his leg again, but said nothing. She just laughed. Leif had no idea how to respond to her. She had continued to surprise him from the moment she greeted him just two minutes earlier.

Jan came down from her laughing fit with another happy sigh. "That was good. Truth and lies bring their own delightful humor, don't you think? Anyway. What *are* you searching for Leif," she said, in a mock sage voice.

Leif paused a beat, unsure if this was a set up for a joke. But it appeared Jan had had her laughs and was actually curious now about why he was stumbling into her yard late on a cold November night.

"A deer," he said.

"Ahhh. Always the deer. Any old deer? You just had to see one before bedtime?"

"No, actually. *The* deer, I guess you could say. There's been a monster sighted in the area, and I kind of really want to be the one who…" He considered which word to use. "Finds it."

"A monster, you say?"

"I just mean a really big one. A one-in-a-million type deal."

"I see. And you thought you might find it in your yard or my yard in the middle of the night?"

"No, that's not what I mean. I just want to find it – hopefully tomorrow morning – and so that's making it tough to sleep tonight."

Jan nodded, thinking on what he was saying.

"And so, since you can't find this deer, and since you're afraid you *won't* find this deer, you're looking for something else that might take your mind off it – something meaningful you can find instead?"

Leif shrugged. "Sure. I guess that's a way of saying it. Better than I would have said it."

Jan nodded again and stared out across the moonlit yard.

Leif looked out too and waited for her to say something more, but she didn't. Then he remembered what she had said the first time he met her.

"And, what is it that *you're* looking for?"

She waited a moment before responding, continuing to look out into the darkness.

"Sometimes I just like to sit outside."

It was a disappointing answer. Perhaps it was a fair one, but Leif had a feeling she didn't sit out late on a cold night just because she liked the fresh air.

"There are two things I should tell you, Leif. The first is that I was serious when I said I'm gay. Sorry for laughing at your expense – it just came out. Pun not intended. But yes, I am. The second thing is that I'm sorry about the other day with the leaves and the phone call. I couldn't explain it to you then, but I'm sure that was awkward and uncomfortable for you."

"Oh, it's okay. Both things, don't worry about either of them."

There was an extended silence, but Leif could tell she was about to say more.

"You seem like a good man, Leif. And maybe I should tell you what it is I'm looking for, or what it is that sometimes seems like it's looking for me, and what brings me out on nights like this. And maybe I will. But I can and will tell you this, because it concerns the phone call and the joke, both made at your expense: I was on the phone with my father, and I am a gay woman, and the two are related."

Leif nodded slowly, feeling he had gained some understanding.

Jan stood up from the step, and Leif took that as a cue to do the same.

"Let's make a deal, Leif. No, a pact. You will continue to ask me questions, and I will continue to ask you questions, and we will both answer as we see fit, so long as we are always honest. Do we have a deal? Or, fuck, sorry – too long in the business world – is it a *pact*? Are we agreed?"

She extended her hand. Leif took it and they shook.

"Agreed."

Jan smiled and started up the steps onto the deck. Leif was about to turn to go but stopped.

"Jan?"

She turned.

"I would like to put this pact into practice now, and I would like to ask: do you have any family in the area? Or would you…" Leif was about to extend hospitality he normally didn't make a point of extending. "Would you like to join me and my family for Thanksgiving?"

Jan smiled, but it was a pained smile. "The answer to both questions is yes."

Leif cocked his head. "Well, that's great then. I'll let you know. But…you *do* have family in the area?"

Jan sighed, smiled, and shrugged.

"Damn this pact already. Yes. Yes I do. But I won't be with them. Now good-night, Leif."

She turned and went inside.

"Goodnight, Jan."

Twelve: Girl in the Woods

Lily Huang parked her decrepit Chevy at the end of the barnyard where the gravel gave way into a muddy field. It was early – more than an hour before daylight – but Mr. Leonardson was already up in the barn with the dairy cows. Lily was no stranger to early mornings with swim team practice and jazz band, but to be up working in the barn year in and year out just to make it on a small dairy farm was borderline insane. Mr. Leonardson was a kind man. He was older and all his kids had moved out, and now he and his wife were always looking for ways to be involved with the kids in their parish. It had taken the 13-year-old Lily weeks to work up the nerve to ask Mr. Leonardson after Mass one day if she could hunt on his land, and, to her relief, his eyes had lit up as he said yes. Now, four years later, she knew every inch of the forty acres of fields and forest. She had harvested three does and a six-point buck. And she was comfortable and friendly around Mr. and Mrs. Leonardson, though she still minded her p's and q's and called ahead every time she came out for a hunt.

She stepped out of the truck and into the cold. It was getting late in the year and overnight temperatures were dropping and dropping. She was thankful for her new gloves her cousin Minh gave her for her birthday. She had saved a lot of money to buy a warm blaze orange jacket, but had found that by the end of a hunt it was always her fingers and toes which had suffered the worst.

She closed the door of her truck and winced at the rattling sound it made. It was a shitty truck, but it ran, and she had gotten more than a fair price for it. She had college expenses on the horizon – and a nicer vehicle could wait longer than adequate protection from the frigid temperatures of Badger Creek.

She opened the back door and slid the hard-shell gun case across the seat towards her. She opened it and removed her father's semi-automatic .30-06 and slung it over her shoulder. Most people would say it was too big for her, but it was the only rifle she had ever known. The first time she took it to the range, the recoil overpowered her and the scope struck her in the forehead and left a lump. But she didn't turn gun-shy, and she had become a skilled shooter. Still, it was heavy, and she was thankful for the sling, even if it might have looked a little silly resting across the back of her short and slight frame.

The ammo bag was on the floor – which always managed to get filthy – and she procured a magazine of five shells and put it into her coat pocket. There was no sense in loading now, as it was still an hour before shooting was even legal, though she fully expected to hear early shots today.

She double-checked to make sure her back-tag was facing out and that she had her phone, buck knife, chapstick, hand warmers, and snack. All set, she took a deep breath and headed out into the muddy field.

The cold and dry air had turned the ground into hard, crumbling ruts. It was worse when the ground was wet during the bow hunt and last spring when she had tried turkey hunting for the first time. She was used to this ground, and her boots fit her well. It was not easy going, but training for swimming and track all year made it easier for her than most others. She was an age of constant energy, which helped when she had to stay up late to study for a biology exam and then get up early for practice.

She was glad for the light of the moon – which was still high in the sky – so that she could see her way well enough without a flashlight. She didn't want anything to spoil the odds on opening day, especially not this year with talk of The Thirty Pointer. It seemed ridiculous, but she felt she had just as good a chance of taking it as anyone. Why not?

The familiar path to the tree stand brought her to her destination. The stand was of a basic design – a box of wood on top of a platform with a ladder, but had fallen into disrepair after Mr. Leonardson's sons grew up. Lily had used it as she found it the first year, but when one of the ladder steps broke under her foot she decided it was time to fix it up. She did all the research and borrowed all the right equipment, but she found she could only do it with Mr. Leonardson's help, which he happily gave. She had wondered – and still did – what kind of a stand her grandfather could have helped her build. He had dug elaborate tunnels and constructed sturdy fortifications during the war designed to kill other men, so he must have been able to build a stand effective for killing deer.

But she had never asked him for his help. He wouldn't have agreed.

She climbed the ladder, and then slowly opened the door so as to not make a sound and to avoid startling any animals that might be inside. She always closed the door and windows after a hunt, but she couldn't shake the idea that a family of raccoons could still find a way in.

The stand was clear, and she made ready by opening the windows and settling into the old chair she had just refurbished the year before. Then she took the magazine from her pocket and loaded her rifle, setting it in the corner of the stand until legal hunting hours got closer. She looked out the right window, and was satisfied to see that, even though the stand was just inside the tree line, she had a shooting lane. The same was true on the left. Ahead of her was an open field which deer often entered. A quarter mile to the east there was a rock pile which had grown up into a little island in the field, and she sometimes hunted from there. But this morning it would be too cold to go without the little extra warmth the stand afforded. She also felt too exposed on the island, and on opening day she wanted to have at least some element of surprise.

She sat and waited. She checked the time on her phone dozens of times, urging daylight on, but still the hunt would not begin for another five minutes. Hoping to speed time up, she picked up her rifle, shouldered it, resting it on the window ledge, and looked through the scope to scan the distant reaches of her field of view.

There was a gunshot. Early, and close, judging by the sound.

Lily jumped a little, even though she had expected to hear some hunters pushing the legal limits. Her heart raced for a moment, especially because it sounded so close. She liked to feel like she was the only hunter in the woods, and gunshots – especially the close ones – shattered that illusion in an unpleasant way.

Then the legal opening of the season finally arrived, and Lily smiled.

A couple hours passed, and Lily decided it was time for a snack. She was hungry, and while she was trying to relax in the woods, she was finding herself exerting a lot of energy focusing on careful scans of her surroundings. Whether or not that was actually making her hungry, she wasn't sure, but it was a nice excuse for some trail mix.

She always kept her snacks in cloth sacks. Plastic bags and wrappers made too much noise. She procured her bag from a coat pocket and dumped the mix into her hand, going without the glove and braving the chill for just long enough to toss a couple of big handfuls into her mouth. She wanted a drink of water, and normally she had a large bottle with her wherever she went, but she wouldn't be going in until the middle of the day and she wanted to avoid having to go before then.

The middle of the day was soon in coming as the sun climbed in the sky and no deer appeared in the field. She had thought she might have heard one running through the woods behind her, but she couldn't see very far out that window, let alone get a shot.

Somewhat reluctantly, she closed up shop, unloaded her rifle, and climbed down from the stand. It was just about 1 o'clock, and the Leonardsons would be waiting for her to have lunch before she headed back out to get a couple more hours in that afternoon. Normally she worked at Culver's on Saturdays, but she had succeeded in getting this day off. This day was for the hunt.

Opening day yielded no game for Lily. She returned home in the early evening with darkness fully descended. She sighed in satisfaction as she stepped from the garage into the warmth of the house.

"It's me," she called out when no one greeted her.

"In the family room," replied her grandmother.

Lily removed her boots, careful to not get mud anywhere it shouldn't be. Despite the warmth of the house, she was reluctant to lose any more layers, but she had a schedule to keep.

She went to the kitchen in her overalls, sweater, and wool socks. It sounded like the news was on in the family room.

First she poured a tall glass of water from the pitcher in the fridge, and then she hunted for leftovers. She thought there might be some leftover gỏi cuốn, and a couple rolls would be enough to tide her over.

"I made lasagna."

Lily looked up over the door of the fridge to see her grandmother had entered the kitchen.

"Hm?"

"Lasagna. For our dinner." *Lasagna* was a tough word for a woman who had only known Vietnamese until she was 30.

"Oh, sorry. I understood I just…I'm still defrosting," said Lily. "Anyway, I'm going to Mass, so I just wanted to eat something quick before I go. You can eat without me."

"Oh? Mass on Saturdays? Shut the door, please."

"I will, I was just looking for the gỏi cuốn from Thursday. Do you know where it is?" Lily ducked back into the fridge, determined to find it. "And yeah but I'm going hunting tomorrow morning."

"So much hunting. So much Mass. Shut the door please."

"Yeah I will but where's the gỏi cuốn?"

"Gone."

Lily straightened up and then shut the door with an exasperated sigh.

"Stay and eat lasagna."

"I would like to go to Mass." She headed to the pantry for a more accessible snack.

"Your friends won't be there. They go Sundays."

"I'm going to meet a few of them afterwards."

"Oh?"

"Yeah." She grabbed a blueberry toaster strudel and took it over to the toaster. She would be hungry but she could eat some more with her friends.

"Where?"

"Culver's, I think."

"So much Culver's. What time?"

"What time what?" Lily was getting annoyed, and she pushed down the toaster handle with more force than needed.

"Will you be back?"

"I don't know."

"Lily." It was her grandfather's voice. "Your grandmother asked you a simple question."

Lily turned away from the toaster and looked at her grandparents on the other side of the kitchen. They stood next to each other, grandmother with her hands clasped, grandfather with his arms crossed, the TV remote still in his hand, both wearing matching stern looks, both short, wiry thin, with deep gray hair and well-earned wrinkles and liver spots. They were a version of *American Gothic*.

"Maybe 9?"

"That's fine," said her grandmother.

"And where's she going?" said her grandfather.

"To Mass. And then with friends."

"Mass is on Sundays."

"She is hunting tomorrow."

"She was hunting today."

"*She* is right here," said Lily.

The grandparents fixed her with a stare and said nothing. The toaster ejected the strudel with a *clang*. The stare continued. Lily smelled the strudel and turned to get it from the toaster, placing it on a small plate and turning back to her grandparents. Suddenly she felt warm in her cold-weather garb.

Then her grandfather looked aghast. He swore in Vietnamese.

"Your swim meet! We didn't even ask! It was last night!" he swore again.

Her grandmother's face turned into the same look of shock.

"You came back too late and woke up too early. How... how did you do?"

Lily couldn't stop a smile.

"Our relay is going to state."

Both grandparents made joyful exclamations and advanced towards her. They were smiling.

"I knew you would," said her grandmother.

"We knew you would," said her grandfather. "Please forgive two old-timers for having a...a what is it?"

"A senior moment," said Lily.

"That. Yes."

They put their hands on her and patted her on the shoulders.

"We are proud."

"Yes we are."

"Thank you," said Lily, her body getting warmer and her strudel getting colder.

Her grandparents stepped back.

"Well. Yes. Very good. So. Back at 9," said her grandmother, resuming her demeanor but with a lingering smile and twinkle in her eyes.

"Sure. Back at 9."

Thirteen: Thanksgiving

Leif and Jan turned off the county highway towards Leif's parents' house. It was overcast and wet, pasting some uncollected leaves of autumn colors to the pavement. Most days were clear reminders that fall was too soon gone and winter was on the way. But no weather could dampen Thanksgiving – not for Leif's family. No one, save maybe Anders and Mindy, looked towards Christmas until the holiday was over, and wouldn't even think of a Christmas cookie until all the Thanksgiving leftovers had been finished off.

"Why did you invite me to come today?" said Jan.

Leif shrugged.

"Why not?"

"Remember our pact, dear comrade."

Leif laughed and shrugged again.

"I just don't like the thought of my neighbor being alone on Thanksgiving. And, I don't know, maybe it was a little out of nowhere, but we *had* just made a blood oath, and if you can't break bread on a holiday with your fellow oath keepers, well, who can yah do it with?"

Leif halted at a stop sign and waited for a little old woman walking a Newfoundland to cross.

"Oh my – I hope that dog is well-behaved. No chance she'd be able to stop it if it decided to run," said Jan.

"Yeah, that's Mrs. Morgan. She has had Newfies for as long as I can remember. When one dies she gets another. And she's always walked them no problem."

"Oh, I like that," said Jan. Then she laughed a little and shook her head. "A blood oath. You have a good sense of humor Leif. Or at least you make me laugh."

Leif rolled his eyes.

"My mom and sister are always saying how funny I am, but I don't consider myself to be so hilarious. Maybe you'll get along really well with them."

"You *are* funny. Humorous, too," said Jan, winking even though Leif wasn't looking at her. "My brother was the same way. Mom and I laughed at everything he said in his quiet manner."

"Oh, I didn't know you have a brother," said Leif, slowing the truck and pulling over to the side of the road outside his parents' house.

"Yes," said Jan, the mirth gone from her voice.

"Does he live in the area?" said Leif, turning off the truck, not noticing the change in her voice.

"No, he's…"

"Our pact!"

"Look, we're here, yes – this is the place?"

Leif looked at Jan and found that she was not looking at him and instead was fumbling with the door handle.

"Jan?"

"The pact as I understand it is a little more about persisting in asking than in having to answer." She finally got the door ajar but did not swing it open.

"Oh, I know, and so I'm asking, but right now I'm just asking if you're okay?"

Jan paused and took a deep breath.

"Yeah. I'm okay. I just…I have a way of saying things out loud that – if I thought them through – maybe I wouldn't say."

"I think I sometimes have the opposite problem."

"Well, all the more reason for our pact."

Leif nodded and released his seat belt, and Jan took that as a cue to push open her door. They got out and walked up towards the steps past the other cars parked in the driveway. It appeared Leif was last to arrive, which was still well before food would be served or the Packer game would begin.

"My brother is dead. And every day I wish I could laugh at his dry sense of humor."

Leif looked her way, but she stared towards the house, her gaze distant.

"I'm sorry to hear that."

"But I'm glad to have been able to say it."

Leif nodded, satisfied with the glacial rate at which he learned more about Jan.

Jan turned to him as he rang the doorbell (out of habit, since of course he was allowed to just walk in). "Why are you single, Leif?"

He was taken aback. "Oh, no particular reason, and if there was, would I have time to explain that now?"

"No, but now when I ask you again you'll have a better answer ready."

Jan had barely finished speaking when Mary opened the door with a big smile.

"Hi there! Come in, come in!"

Leif hugged his mother. Jan expected a handshake, and she was extending her hand and about to introduce herself when Mary reached out and embraced her. Jan happily returned the hug after a surprised *ope*.

"Oh give me a hug it's Thanksgiving. You must be Jan! I'm Mary."

"Jan I am. Nice to meet you."

"I love your sweater," said Mary, noting Jan's Packers attire. Mary was wearing a Fall-themed cardigan.

"Go Pack go. I like yours – matches this lovely fall theme," said Jan, looking around at the decorations in the entryway.

"Thank you, thank you. Well, come on in, everyone's kinda hanging out and bothering us to get dinner ready faster."

"You and Liz?" said Leif.

"Well, yes, but Doug, too! He's got some special casserole he's been dying to make. But it's taking him forever!"

Mary and Leif began to head in towards the living room.

"Oh, Mary, shoes on or off?" said Jan.

"You can leave them on if you want – finally got hardwood floors everywhere so no problem if we make a mess. All that time cleaning up after Norris and then we get the floors and then he goes and dies."

"But it's okay with you if I take them off?"

"Oh, sure, yes, either way!"

Jan took off her shoes and caught up to Leif, who was following his mother towards the living room where there was the sound of laughter and a giggling baby.

"Who is Norris?"

"Oh, their dog."

"I thought so. Hoped so. A much darker story if they're cleaning up after a man named Norris."

"You know, you have a good sense of humor too."

Jan beamed.

"You're right. I do. Now take me to your leader."

The living room was again filled with all of Leif's local family. The TV was on NFL pregame programming, but everyone's attention was on baby Audrey, sitting on Mindy's lap, staring wide-eyed at the baby talk and cooing of everyone else. Focused as they were, they still turned to notice the arrival of Leif and this stranger.

"Leif!" Marge stood up and greeted her nephew with a hug.

"Hi, Auntie. So, everyone, this is my new neighbor, Jan."

"Hello, everyone."

There was a chorus of *hellos*.

"This is my Aunt Marge and Uncle Doug, my sister's husband, Jason, and their son Luke…"

Leif didn't notice, but Jan's eyes sparkled as she was introduced to the boy.

"…and my father, Clint, and Grandpa Delmar, and my older brother, Anders, and his wife, Mindy, and, the star of the show, Audrey."

Jan was a picture of joy looking at the infant and her mother.

"Thank you, everyone, for allowing me to intrude on your family gathering.

Leif invited me but the acceptance extends to you, and I just…oh, I can't contain myself, may I please hold your baby?"

"Oh, yes, you may…could you wash your hands first?" said Mindy. Then added, "not that I think you're dirty or…"

Jan procured a small bottle of hand sanitizer from her jeans pocket.

"Well, you came prepared!" said Anders.

Jan rubbed the alcohol solution onto her hands. "You shake a lot of hands in the business world. I can't leave home without it."

Anders stood up to give Jan room to sit down next to Mindy. She took the infant into her arms with care and took a moment to stare into Audrey's eyes before engaging in baby talk.

Liz came into the living room and introduced herself to Jan. Her appearance reminded Doug to check on the casserole.

"Don't you mess this up now, Dougie," said Marge.

Doug made a dismissive sound and waved his hand as he hurried into the kitchen.

As was usually the case, conversation centered on the baby. Jan was interested in knowing all about her, and her parents were only too happy to repeat answers they had given many times before. It was several minutes before anyone seemed to remember that a stranger was among them.

"You said you're in business?" said Anders.

"I was. I did financial consulting. But I'm retired."

Audrey started to fuss and Jan handed her back to Mindy, smiling all the while.

"And then you moved into Betty's house just a few months ago?" said Anders.

"Yep, end of September. It's been good, I'm really happy with the house. And the town."

"Ohhhh, this is who moved into Betty's house?" said Jason, who had been half-listening as he had a private conversation with Luke, who was always less interested in the baby than the adults. "You haven't seen The Thirty-Pointer, have you?"

Jan laughed. "So Leif isn't the only one looking for that? No, no, haven't seen it. I don't see many deer on my property, actually. They must be in the woods. Otherwise Leif would just hunt them from my back deck!"

Jason nodded. "Shame."

"You're getting settled into life here, though?" said Mindy.

"Yes, yes. It's peaceful. Which I wanted. Not that Green Bay – where I moved from – was all hustle and bustle – well, who can actually describe that city. A…unique place. But, anyway, this is more peaceful and if I just want to sit at home and relax I can do that. But I'll want to get more connected and involved. I retired too young to sit around all the time."

Marge nodded in agreement.

"Yeah, Doug still works but I retired, and one way I've stayed connected – and I totally know what you mean – is to be involved with our church. Have you found one yet?"

Jan blushed just a little.

"No, I'm Buddhist, and there isn't a temple here – surprise. Not that I would go. I'm a pretty bad Buddhist."

"But you still celebrate Thanksgiving?"

Everyone turned to Clint, who had not spoken since Jan sat down.

Jan cocked her head. "Is Thanksgiving a Christian holiday?"

"It isn't Buddhist."

Jan nodded.

"Touché, that it isn't."

"Dad," said Leif. "It isn't a religious holiday. It's an American holiday."

Clint raised an eyebrow.

"And Jan is American."

Clint nodded knowingly. "I meant no offense."

Anders coughed. "The Pilgrims and the Indians didn't worship the same God, but when they shared a meal on that first Thanksgiving, that didn't matter. They celebrated family and friendship and generosity, and that's what we're doing here today…" and then, raising his voice a little. "If Doug ever finishes his casserole!"

Jan laughed with everyone else but then leaned towards Anders and grasped his wrist. "Ah, wise words, young man." She looked from Anders, to Leif, to Clint, and back to Anders with an intent gaze. "But we do, in fact, worship the same God. And his name…" she turned to the TV and smiled "…is Brett Favre."

Everyone turned and half cheered, half laughed as they found the Packers' quarterback warming up on the TV.

"He's been on fire," said Marge.

"As good as ever," said Jason.

Luke just beamed looking at his hero.

"But do you still say Bart Starr is the best Packers quarterback ever, Grandpa?" said Anders.

Grandpa Delmar, sitting quiet in the recliner, smiled and shrugged. "Favre's a throwback," he said in a soft voice. "But I throw way back."

Attention remained on the pregame, even though everyone was really thinking about the food they could smell so well by now.

"Hope this gets done soon," said Clint. "Game isn't too far off now. Game's serious business, and eating Thanksgiving dinner is serious business. Can't divide the attention. Not with this meal." He was serious, but it was said in jest.

"Oh yah, you're right on that one there," said Marge.

Leif nodded in full agreement.

"Leif says you all get together on a lot of game days," said Jan, mostly directing her statement towards Clint. "I think that's great. My parents never understood the fascination with football. So the rest of us would make game days our thing. And we'd tailgate a couple times a year when I got tickets through work."

Leif wondered who exactly Jan meant by *we*.

"Well like you said, it's like religion around here," said Clint. "Which people are also pretty serious about. Religion," he said, stealing a quick glance at Leif. "So your parents must not be from around here?"

Clint was a careful talker. Leif knew his father had just found a way to ask Jan where she was from without asking it – while rebuking him for not going to church to boot. He was sure Jan must have picked up on it too, but she didn't give anything away.

"No, not originally. Though they have lived in the Green Bay area for most of their lives. They're from Vietnam."

Clint raised his eyebrows. "Oh. I've been there."

Jan nodded. "I know."

There was the briefest of awkward silences when Mary entered the living room and announced that the dinner was ready. She didn't have to tell anyone twice.

It was a fantastic spread of food which met everyone's approval. While it had held up proceedings, Doug's casserole was a hit and all was forgiven. Luke wasn't sure at first if the strange looking pile of food was safe to approach, but he found it to be much to his liking. He was seated close enough to Jan that she could have a few somewhat private words with him as Anders and Doug carried the conversation on the other end of the table for a few minutes.

"You're seven, right Luke?"

He nodded, accepting that adults just know things.

"And you always get to sit at the grown-up table?"

"The grown-up table?"

Jan smiled. He had never even heard of *the kids' table*.

"Sometimes the kids sit at a table by themselves. But some kids, like you, and like my niece, are the only kid, so they always have to...or maybe *get to* sit with the grown-ups. But not all of them eat the grown-up food." She nodded towards his cleaned plate.

Leif was sitting next to Jan. He was listening in and trying to map out a family tree.

"Oh," said Luke. "Well, I like Grandma's food."

"It's very good, yes. The next step now is sharing in the adult conversation. That can be even harder to try than casserole."

As if to prove her point, Luke seemed a little confused.

"Yeah. I do wish I had a brother though."

If his parents heard they pretended not to. Leif winced internally.

"Not a sister?" said Jan.

Luke frowned. "I wouldn't want to play with her."

"Oh, you might say that. I wasn't sure how I felt about getting a little brother, but we ended up playing together and having fun all the time."

Leif continued to work out the family tree as the meal progressed.

"Well, Mary, and Liz, and Doug, I have to say – and I really mean I *have* to say – that this is a marvelous meal," said Jan.

The others added their approval.

"Why, thank you, Jan."

"And Jan knows," said Leif. "She's a great cook."

"You don't need to know how to cook to know great food!" said Jason, patting his stomach, which was just beginning to develop.

"True," said Jan. "And Leif is too kind. But I do cook, and I used to help my mother with cooking on big family gatherings, and I know how tricky it can be to balance so many dishes at once."

"Well, I had good helpers," said Mary. Then, looking at Liz, "Or at least one good helper." She winked at Doug.

"If you don't mind my asking," said Liz, "what kind of food would you make on Thanksgiving with your family? Did you make these kinds of things?"

"Yes, my mother learned a lot of American cooking and we'd make your classic turkey and stuffing type things for Thanksgiving. But we didn't always have too many people over on Thanksgiving. Christmas was sort of a strange hodge-podge because my brother converted to Catholicism when he married, and so it was sort of religious, sort of Santa, sort of Vietnamese…but the big one, when we got together with anyone even remotely related to us, was Tết."

Leif stole a glance at his father. He didn't react to the word or give away what it meant to him.

"That's like a New Year's celebration, right?" said Liz.

"Yes, but much bigger than New Year's celebrations are in America. It's the big one in Vietnam. And we'd go all out Fresh Off the Boat for that one. My mother and I worked and worked to get that ready. It meant so much to her that even when I'd make a mistake she'd just be so happy to be doing it, she never got angry." She sighed. "I loved doing that. Making food for others is just…well you know. It's the best. So I know why Doug insisted on entering the lists."

"It was my pleasure," said Doug, raising his glass of hard apple cider.

Anders raised his glass. "To Uncle Doug and his casserole!"

To Uncle Doug and his casserole.

Leif smiled, but his mind was on a family tree and the cold expression on his father's face.

His thoughts remained so occupied until the plates were cleared and it was time to watch the game. Doug floated the idea of serving up pie right away, but Mary insisted the dinner must settle and she'd dish it up during halftime. Doug protested for a moment, but Jan grabbed him by the arm.

"Come along now, Chef Douglas – our champions take to the field. Missing kick-off is bad luck!"

Doug looked down at her and smiled.

"That's what I always say!"

And the two of them hurried off to the living room, pie forgotten for the moment as the coin toss concluded and the game began.

Leif and Jan were in the truck again, headed back out to their homes. Darkness had fallen and the cold set in, and both were ready to lie around for a little while before going to sleep.

"So…did you enjoy your time?" said Leif.

"I did! Very much so. Your family is very kind and a lot of fun."

"Good, good."

"And the food, of course. Fantastic. I'm so glad I got that pecan pie recipe from your mother."

"Oh that's my favorite."

"And of course the Packers won. So, yeah, that was a great time."

"Yeah…"

Jan stifled a yawn and turned towards Leif.

"What is it?"

"I'm just sorry about my dad. Some of the things he hinted at."

Jan waved her hand.

"I'm sure it seemed more awkward to you, being the one who invited me. It was no big deal, really."

"Really? Well, if you say so."

They rode in silence for a minute or two.

"Is that what he was like with your girlfriends? Is that why you don't have one?" Jan asked the question she had promised with a smile.

Leif laughed.

"No, he was always nice to my girlfriends. Mom was too, actually."

Jan nodded. "My question still stands."

Leif shrugged.

"My previous answer does too, I guess. There's not a particular reason. It just hasn't happened for me yet. Though it would be nice to get people to stop bothering me about it."

"Ah, yes, so many see singleness as a curse. I don't think you do. But you almost seem resigned to it."

Leif made a face.

"What do you mean? How…how could you know that?"

"I don't know exactly how I know. Or think I know. But it seems like you set aside the desire for partnership so you don't miss it when you don't have it."

Leif said nothing. He had the odd sensation that someone was reading him the pages of a book he'd read and since forgotten.

"Let me ask you this, Leif. Do you imagine ways your life could be better?"

Leif shifted, his defenses bristling a little.

"I like the way my life is."

Jan nodded.

"Yes, yes, I'm not saying you don't. And that's good. But…okay, let me ask you this – did you like the way your life was in high school? Or in college?"

Leif thought for a moment back on his days in high school as a popular person, successful athlete, and capable student. He thought about college and the fun he had and the success he found, as well as the way those things had given way to restlessness and his decision to leave.

"Yes. For the most part."

"But did you, even as you liked the way things were, think about how things could be better? Like did you find a way to enjoy your life and be satisfied and content while also working towards something else or aspiring to something that seemed bigger and better?"

Leif thought again for a moment. It was a hard question, but the answer seemed fairly obvious given what happened.

"Yes. And then, when I tried to do that thing, it didn't work out."

Jan relaxed into her seat and looked out the side window.

"That's what I thought."

They drove on in silence. Leif wanted desperately to ask about Jan's family after the clues he had picked up during the day, but it didn't seem appropriate right at the moment. Perhaps enough weight had been carried for one day.

By the time they arrived, both of them were back in lighter spirits. Leif pulled over to the side of the road to let Jan out in front of her house – she had jibed him about wanting to pull all the way into the driveway just to back out and pull into his.

"Thank you again, Leif. This was a really great day. I'm going to sleep well to-night, I think."

"Me too."

"Gonna be up early looking for The Thirty-Pointer?"

"Oh yah. Time is growing short."

"Yes. Well, I wonder if the deer sees it that way. If he sees things like that. In any way. Anyway…good night, good luck, and be safe out there."

"Thank you, Jan. Bye now."

Jan shut the truck door and headed up the driveway. She had hardly made it to the door before Leif felt alone.

Fourteen: Biology

Lily arrived early to her first class of the day, AP Biology. She could have slept in, since there was no Jazz Band rehearsal and the swimmers were tapering their workouts for the state meet, but her internal alarm clock wouldn't let her, and so she arrived at school well before the first bell. A handful of other students were sitting around Mr. Lambert's classroom. Three of her junior classmates were lounging in some desks across the aisle from her – Cole, Jackson, and Trevor. They happened to be catching up on their weekend hunts.

"Two more does for me," said Cole.

"Two? How many is that now?" said Jackson.

"Six."

"Wait, what?" said Trevor. "You've shot six does? This year?"

"Yeah. For Earn a Buck – the older guys at my hunting cabin let me shoot them and then they tag them so they can go for bucks." He shrugged, sinking deeper into his slouching position.

"That's stupid," said Jackson.

"Good for the older guys," said Trevor. "Kinda smart, actually."

"I don't mind it. They let me claim the first one, so I can still get my buck if I see one."

"It's stupid," said Jackson, his voice and expression lazy, or at least sleepy. "Who wants to shoot a bunch of does all weekend?"

Cole shrugged again.

"Well you have to shoot at least one for the buck," said Trevor.

"Oh, shit, really, is that how that works?" said Jackson. He rolled his eyes. "I got mine in the bowhunt."

"No buck?" said Trevor.

"No. I passed on a couple of eight pointers."

"Screw you," said Trevor. "I need to hunt where you hunt. I'd shoot an eight pointer."

"I was passing on anything small."

"Eight points isn't small," said Trevor.

"It's because this idiot thought he was going to shoot The Thirty Pointer," said Cole.

"Hey, with everyone looking for it – like even people who have never hunted in their life – I thought there's no way it survives the season. I've only got one buck tag. If I was going to get it, this would be the year."

"Well, looks like we're all going to get another chance. Should've taken the eight pointer" said Trevor.

Lily scanned over the pages of her textbook, but focused more on their conversation. She never got to talk hunting with anyone. None of her friends were hunters, and she wasn't sure if anyone at school even knew she hunted. These boys weren't who she would have wanted to talk with anyway. In her eyes, they were like most high school boys: some combination of loud, rude, arrogant, aggressive, and ignorant. Or, as her cousin Minh had said once, *young, dumb, and full of cum*. Boys and young men like them – especially white ones – made her nervous. She thought some people might say she was unfair, but she was always distrustful of red-blooded American boys.

Red-blooded American boys had taken so much from her.

She did, however, think Cole might have a good perspective on things. There was nothing shameful or small about killing does, as long as someone got to eat them. What he was doing might have been a little cheap, but it wasn't wasteful. Lily wanted to shoot The Thirty Pointer as much as anyone, and then she would make sure people at school knew all about it, but she wasn't in it just for the trophies.

As the start of class approached and more students filed in, Lily's friend Carmen settled into the desk in front of her.

"Hey swim star! How's my little Michelle Phelps?" said Carmen. She was one of the few people who was as tireless as Lily.

"Heyyy," said Lily. "I'm good. How was your weekend at the cottage?"

"Fun! Oh my gosh you should have gone! You would've had fun."

"Yeah, I bet it was good. But the meet and stuff…"

"It was so cold! But it's like a nice cabin so it was warm. And Will was there – you could've snuggled up with him."

Lily blushed. "Stahhhhp."

"Well, did you have a nice Thanksgiving at least?"

"Yeah it was good."

"Did you have a lot of family over?"

"I just had a meal with my grandparents. We don't have any other family who are that close. But I went over to a church friend's house later."

"Oh fun. We had a pretty chill Thanksgiving too. Which was okay since the weekend got a little craaaaazy."

Lily smiled. She wasn't so sure the weekend at the cabin sounded any better than her weekend in the woods, even if she had also missed out on getting a buck this year.

By now Mr. Lambert had arrived and begun writing some things on the board. The bell rang, and students found their seats.

Mr. Lambert began class with some obligatory remarks about turkey, tryptophan, and leftovers. Then he brought up their last test.

"I did finally finish grading your last tests. Sorry that took so long. And, since I've told you that, and since I know you'll just be wanting to find out all class instead of focusing on what I can assure you will be a riveting lecture, I'll hand them back and go over the answers now."

There were murmurs of approval as he retrieved a stack of papers from his desk and began returning them to students.

"Overall the scores were pretty good," said the teacher. "I was pleased, although it's obvious we need to go over a few things again that almost all of you got wrong. But they were pretty good. No perfect scores, but there was one 98."

A 98 was high, but Lily thought there was a chance it might be her. And, when Mr. Lambert arrived at her desk and placed her stapled test in front of her, she allowed herself a smile when she turned the papers over and found a 98 circled at the top.

Students started comparing scores and whispers rose to a dull roar as Mr. Lambert continued to return the tests. Carmen received hers and then stole a glance back at Lily's.

"Are you freaking kidding me? How are you so good at everything?"

Lily blushed again, feeling a surge of pride and embarrassment.

"I ask myself that sometimes," she said, allowing herself a moment to boast. Then she added with a serious face, "No, but actually you just have to be Asian."

Carmen laughed – a little too freely, Lily noted.

"And I know you study a lot too, so there's just no chance for me."

"The studying a lot comes with being Asian. And living with mean old Asians."

Carmen laughed the same laugh, and Lily decided the ironic joke had run its course for the time being.

"So are your grandparents super strict with grades and stuff with college just a couple years away?"

Lily shrugged.

"They're not as mean as I make it seem. They just want me to be my best. And they already raised two smart kids so they think they've got the system down. But, yeah, they would kill…" the word caught in Lily's throat, but Carmen didn't notice. "…I mean disown…" that word wasn't better, and she winced. Carmen raised an eyebrow. "They *really* want me to get into a good college. I don't think they care what I study so long as I get a respectable and high-paying job."

Carmen nodded, but didn't respond as Mr. Lambert started to quiet the class down and began reviewing answers.

Lily sighed, her excellent score forgotten for the moment. It seemed less significant as she was reminded of the people with whom she so wished she could share in her successes. But they were gone. And no amount of high scores and trophies could bring them back.

Fifteen: The Bar, Again

November turned to December, and the snows began to fall. Leif had a little more of his time occupied working snow removal, but his days off were more empty than ever with most of his favorite hunting seasons come and gone. Once the ice was thicker he would start to go ice fishing more often, but that time had not arrived. With the heavy eating of Thanksgiving and Christmas season arriving, he had meant to get back into his habits of exercising by running or playing basketball at the YMCA, but he was finding it too easy to sit around the house. So much of his life, especially in the military, had been organized around what he was compelled to do by others rather than what he wanted to do. Now, if something felt like something he *should* do rather than wanted to do, he convinced himself he had the right to just not do it. And so he played Xbox and watched TV and read long novels and cleaned hunting equipment. He realized one day it was not so dissimilar from how he killed time in Afghanistan, and the irony was not lost on him.

A habit he did take up again was smoking, and, despite the cold, he stepped out four or five times a day for a cigarette. He knew it was stupid, but trying to be smart all the time was exhausting.

Late in the afternoon of a cold December day, he stepped out his back door for a smoke. He had just taken a couple of drags when Jan – bundled up in an oversized parka – pushed her way through the evergreens and trudged through the snow towards him.

"Hello, Leif," she said as she approached him.

"Hey, Jan."

She arrived at his side and fumbled in her jacket pocket for a moment before procuring a pack of cigarettes. "Got a light?"

Leif was taken aback but reached into his pocket for his lighter.

"I didn't know you smoke."

"I quit a while ago but started again recently. Like you, right?"

Leif nodded.

"I know you can't see me over in my yard, but I see out here sometimes from my window, and I've meant to join you – because smoking is better together – but I'm not going to frantically throw on all my winter garb just to run over here before you duck back inside. But I was just about to go out myself when I espied you."

Leif clicked on the lighter and Jan bent towards it, shielding the flame from the light wind.

"Why did you start again?" said Leif.

Jan shrugged.

"Why does anyone?"

"A fair question, but I'm not just asking about anyone."

Jan laughed.

"Very well, very well, you're good at this." She took a long drag. "Some combination of boredom and the stress that comes from boredom. Something like that."

"I thought you were trying to stay busy?"

"Yes, well, as I'm sure you know, that's not always so easy now is it?"

"Ah, you have me there. I guess you've noticed I'm around most of the day."

"I have. Which I can because, well, I'm around most of the day too."

They continued to smoke, both a little embarrassed that the other was aware of how much time they were spending at home, and that they had both given in to an old habit.

"Hey," said Jan. "When we finish these, instead of going back inside and sitting around for the rest of the day, let's go to the bar."

Leif immediately put his smoke into the snow-filled bowl he used as an ashtray.

"What are we waiting for? Beer is better than tobacco."

Jan laughed and put out her cigarette.

"Especially in Wisconsin winter. Let's go."

They arrived at The Inn right in the middle of Happy Hour. The bar was busy, as many locals stopped by for a couple-two-tree after work, huddled together in the warmth of the tavern, sheltered from a world becoming colder every moment of every day. Classic rock and the din of happy voices floated above the bar décor and the rustic furnishings to give it a cheer befitting the season.

Leif and Jan entered just behind an older man with thick glasses which fogged up when he stepped into the warmth. The man stopped for a moment, blinded, trying to see around the outside of the frames, which made him strike comical poses, like a pelican staring down his bill into the water. Leif and Jan stifled laughs as the man finally removed his glasses and dried them on his Carhartt before trundling off to find a seat.

"Where should we sit?" said Leif.

"Let's go right up to the bar," said Jan.

First, they hung their outer layers on a coat stand. Jan got a good look at Leif's scarf, which was checkered black, white, and gray, and appeared of a high silk quality.

"I like your scarf. It looks…is it from Afghanistan?"

"Oh, yes, thank you. I wore it a lot over there. It's really high quality."

Leif folded the scarf and tucked it into one of his coat pockets.

"Makes a lovely souvenir."

"Yeah…of sorts."

They turned from the hanger and moved towards the bar.

"Not Marine issue, is it?"

Leif shook his head.

"It was…left to me."

He didn't know why he didn't just say who gave it to him and why. It wasn't something he told people, but he was making a habit of telling Jan things he would normally leave unsaid. Not everything needed to be said.

"The…spoils of war, then? I'm not judging, I'm just curious."

"Oh, no, no nothing like that," said Leif, expressing genuine surprise in his eyes as they sat down at the bar. He had never taken anything off a body. "Or, I guess it *is* something like that, since the previous owner died. A guy in my platoon found out he had pancreatic cancer while we were deployed. He left it to me when he was taken home."

"I'm sorry to hear that Leif."

"Yeah, thanks."

Leif stared at the coaster on the bar in front of him, looking at but not really seeing the Leinenkugel's artwork. Jan watched to see if he was about to say something, or if he was cognizant of the bartender walking their way.

"Hey there Leif," said the bartender.

Leif turned his attention to the man, not like he had been startled, but like he was emerging, drowsy, from a nap.

"Hey, Rick. Spotted Cow on tap, yeah?"

"Wouldn't be Happy Hour without it."

"Very good."

"Make that two," said Jan. "And I've got our tab."

Rick raised an eyebrow, seeming to just notice her.

"Yeah she's with me," said Leif. "This is my neighbor, Jan."

Rick smiled and nodded. "Coming right up."

Jan was about to say something when Leif, staring off again, went on.

"It's just things like that, you know? The guy signs his life away to fight in a war, doesn't shoot or get shot at a single time, and then finds out he has one of the most deadly cancers there is. And then dies when he's 22 years old. Just…absurd."

Jan put her hand on his arm and he turned to look at her. She smiled.

"It *is* still a lovely scarf."

He smiled, too, not sure why that sentiment helped untangle his thoughts from the grief of smothered youth.

"It is."

Rick brought their glasses over and they promptly raised them.

"To your friend, gone too soon," said Jan.

"To Miguel," said Leif, his voice catching.

They both took long drinks.

Leif felt a heavy hand slap him on the shoulder.

"Hey there guy."

It was Logan. Chris was with him, too.

"Hey guys."

"I haven't run into you since hunting season, have I? You didn't see that deer out there, did you? I figured if you had that would've been game over."

"Nope, didn't see it."

Jan leaned into the conversation.

"Is this that same deer you're talking about? Is that all anyone talks about?"

Logan looked at her the same way Rick had, surprised to have been addressed by her.

Leif interceded.

"This is my neighbor, Jan. Jan, Logan and Chris."

"Oh nice to meet you," said Logan. Chris nodded with a smile.

"Nice to meet you," said Jan. "And, going to go out on a limb and guess you're wondering if my land is the hunting land or whatever, and yes – yes Leif thinks the majestic Thirty Pointer is roaming around my forest."

Logan's eyes twinkled as he nodded in mock reverence.

"Well you're keeping an eye out for it then, right?"

"Oh, of course."

"All Leif needs is to see it. If he can see it, he can kill it." Logan slapped Leif on the shoulder again. Leif didn't seem comfortable with the line of conversation.

"He was a sniper, you know," said Chris.

"No, I didn't."

Leif realized Logan and Chris had been at the bar for a while already. He wasn't sure where this conversation was going, and his mind raced to find a way to change the subject.

"What's the farthest shot you ever made?" said Logan.

Leif took a drink.

"Close to two miles," he said.

"Holy fuck. And you make the kill?"

Leif shook his head as his face grew warm.

"It was on the practice range."

"Oh, I thought you knew what I meant. What about not at the range?"

Leif took another drink.

"Not far. I always wait for them to get close. There's actually more skill in that, if you ask me. Clean kill, don't spoil the meat, too."

Jan's eyes widened.

"No, no, not a deer. You know what I'm asking. Or I thought you did. Stop being modest, mister sniper. Just between you and me, how far you get one. No bullshit now."

Leif sighed.

"Guys, maybe Leif doesn't want to talk about that," said Jan.

Logan ignored her.

"Come on," he said.

Leif looked Logan in the eye, his stare ice, the other man's face round and ruddy and disturbingly innocent.

"Get the fuck out of my face Logan or I swear to God you'll find out what I can do from close range."

Logan's eyes widened and he stepped back.

"Jesus Christ, Leif. Okay, okay, geez."

Chris tapped Logan on the shoulder and gestured for them to leave.

"Sensitive subject, I guess," said Logan.

"You could've guessed," said Jan.

Logan ignored her and turned away towards where he had been sitting before.

"Sorry about that," said Chris before following.

Again, Leif stared off and Jan waited for him to make the next move. He shifted in his chair, almost like he was going to get up and leave. But he didn't. Instead, he turned to Jan with a hurt expression, a painful look that strained against uncertainty and suffering.

"I never fired my weapon in combat. I never shot at somebody. Not once during my entire tour of duty."

Jan returned a softer version of his look. She could have asked for him to go on, but she knew enough about soldiers and war to guess at the complicated feelings this must create for her neighbor, especially considering his father's experience. And any cliché words of solace or encouragement were sure to sound trite.

"The living and the dead both have long reaches indeed, and each haunts us in turn. What is and what isn't, does and doesn't, will and won't…it is a cruel stroke of fate sometimes which brings us to bear the weight of both."

Leif gave a wry smile.

"Yeah. Well, fuck it."

Jan disapproved of his dismissiveness, real or feigned, but let it go given the circumstance.

"Yeah. Well, I'm hungry. Get that white guy over here and let's order some tater tots and a big pretzel and I don't know what else."

Leif looked around with disinterest, then smiled, as if remembering something half-forgotten, and signaled to Rick the bartender.

"That white guy?"

"No, dummy, the other white guy."

Leif hesitated. "Oh, um…"

"Yes that white guy! I'm kidding you."

Jan shoved his shoulder, her eyes sparkling with a buzz and a tease.

Rick approached them.

"Rick, I need an order of tater tots and an order of cheese curds," said Leif, looking over towards Jan, "and a…"

"And your biggest pretzel," said Jan, leaning towards Rick.

"Sounds good," said Rick, turning to put the order in.

"And bring some beer cheese sauce if you've got it – and I know you do!" Jan called after him.

Leif seemed to relax as he sat back from the bar a little and took a drink.

"Got a story for you," said Jan.

"Let me hear it."

"About Khoi, my brother."

"Oh," said Leif, his voice sinking, and taking a hurried sip of his beer.

"No, no. You're so sweet. Not that kind of story. It's a funny story. Or at least I think it is."

"Ah, okay. Go ahead. Better be funny now."

"Yikes no pressure there. Okay, okay, so, years ago, when I was…how old? Oh it doesn't matter – we were both little. Our dog, Spot…"

"Original name."

"Eff you. Don't interrupt."

"Sorry."

"Our dog, Spot, who was one in a million and a very special good boy, came into the yard with a rabbit in his jaws. Which was horrifying, because he didn't normally kill animals or pick up dead ones. But he brings this rabbit over to us and he just sets it at our feet. I want to go in to get Mom to help us bury it, but Khoi thinks that the rabbit is one of our neighbors' – they kept a few pet rabbits. Not only that, he points out that there are no wounds on the rabbit, so he thinks it isn't dead. But I told him that was dumb – it probably wasn't one of our neighbors', and rabbits don't play dead. Only opossums. But he isn't sure – he's determined that rabbits might do it, too. So I decided to go along with him, but both of us were too afraid to go talk to an adult who we didn't really know, and plus if Spot *had* killed it we didn't want them to know. So we took it to their backyard and sure enough there was an empty cage and we put the rabbit back and left.

"A couple hours later we hear the neighbor lady *screaming* in the backyard. Mom goes over there to see what is wrong – and also to tell her to quiet down – and we go with her, and when my mom asks her what's wrong, the lady says in a panic: 'This rabbit died yesterday and we buried it in the yard and now it's back in the cage!'"

Leif shouted in laughter and it continued to rumble out of him as Jan laughed at a story that had given her joy for many years, and the pain of loss and the darkness of memories faded away as Jan and Leif turned their attention to food and drink and friendship.

Happy Hour came and went, their food had arrived and been eaten, the temperature outside continued to plummet, and still Jan and Leif talked and laughed. But, finally, and only when they were good and ready, Leif suggested they head out.

"Gotta keep up our strength for another day of sitting around, you know," he said. They had enough to drink that the dark joke was funny. "Let's hope our coats are still there."

Jan caught him by the sleeve.

"Leif, you can't drive."

Leif blinked in confusion. No one had told him that in years – if ever.

"You think I'm drunk?"

"Yes, of course you're drunk. I'm drunk."

"You're not driving and I weigh twice as much as you."

"And you had twice as much to drink."

Leif waved his hand.

"You were keeping up. And anyway I have a high tolerance. Let's go."

He turned away to get his coat and Jan grabbed him by the arm again, harder this time.

"Leif! You can't! Just call Anders or someone and have them come get us."

Leif's smile dissipated. Jan's insistence that he couldn't drive seemed an affront to his constitution.

"Jan, don't be silly. I've done this before. I'll just drive carefully. You can close your eyes and sleep until we – ."

Jan slapped him on the cheek.

"Don't you fucking condescend like that to me, Leif. You're drunk and you're not driving."

A few people had noticed the slap and kept their eyes on the two of them. The slight red mark on Leif's face disappeared as he blushed in embarrassment. He wrenched his arm from Jan's grip and headed for the door. Jan followed.

They put their coats on in silence, and Leif wondered if Jan had let it go. She couldn't physically stop him. Dressed, they headed out into the cold.

"I won't go with you, Leif. Please don't go. Just call someone. Or even wait a couple more hours. We can order more tots or cheese curds."

They stood in the entryway, the warmth quickly leaving their bodies in the night chill.

"Jan, what is the big deal? I can drive myself home. And you'd be fine coming with me but if you want I can find someone in there who would be willing to take you, I'm sure."

"The deal is that you're drunk, whether you want to admit it or not, I mean, that's why we sat at a bar for hours, was to use a drug to change our mood and that drug also impairs your ability to drive and why am I having to explain this to you. I mean what the fuck, Leif? People die like this. People die in their cars. They get killed by people, by people like you."

"People like me?" Leif's voice was angry.

"I mean drunk drivers. People who are driving and drunk. And one of them killed my sister-in-law."

Leif was still angry, but he had to take a moment to pause. He hadn't known about this. Drunk as he was, he knew not to trample her personal hurt.

"I was in the car behind her, Leif. I watched it happen. She was dead by the time I got to her, and I still wake up in the night trying to shake those images from my mind. It was a young man, a little older than you, drunk, headed home, who made a reckless mistake. The same mistake you're about to make, whether or not you shatter someone's life on the highway."

Jan's entire body was quivering in hurt and anger. Leif's own aggression evaporated, and his breathing slowed, and his expression softened. There was a long moment of silence, broken only by a man leaving the bar and awkwardly stepping between them. The moment lasted until the sound of the man's boots crunching on the salted sidewalk faded.

"You're right, Jan. You're right. And I'm sorry. And I'm sorry that happened to you. I didn't know."

Jan took a few deep breaths and calmed down as well.

"So you'll call someone?"

Leif nodded.

"Yeah. Yeah I'll call Uncle Doug. No, actually, he might be drunk, too. Maybe. I'll call Liz."

Jan nodded.

"Thank you, Leif. Really." She shivered. "Let's go back inside." She turned to go without waiting for him, but he was right behind her.

They re-entered the shelter of the tavern and waited for Liz in warmth. Outside, the snow began to drift down from heaven. Faintly falling, like fading whispers, on both the living and the dead.

Sixteen: In Concert

Life went on, as it does. The winter in Badger Creek was like many of the winters before it – long, cold, and snowy. Christmas was happy for many, sad for some, busy for most. Businesses closed up or reduced their hours, and some older folks fled south for the winter. College kids came to visit and left again, children continued to go to school before the sun rose and went home after it set. And while some things grow and change even in the winter, and while the smallest units of time are, for some, turbulent and volatile, the march of history in a small town in Wisconsin has a way of consuming it all, especially in the deep dark of winter. Emergent voices and fading lights both blend into the background of melts and freezes, of succession and procession, death and life. And any individual strand which meets a great moment of unraveling finds its way rolled back into the ball of yarn lazily spinning on a wheel of time, until January of 2008 becomes no different from January of 2007 from the grand view of all.

As it turned out, January of 2008 was marked for some significance by one of the darkest days in Packers history, when the green and gold were defeated on their own frozen field by the New York Giants in the game that would have sent them to the Super Bowl, a game that would turn out to be Brett Favre's final one with the team. Jan joined Leif and his family for that game. It was an unhappy time, even if the family and Jan enjoyed one another's company. And there is a special bond that can be created in going through an ordeal such as that.

Leif and Jan did not see much of each other besides that. They both let their best-laid plans and good intentions go to waste, spending most of the winter huddled in their homes, sometimes venturing to the local library or coffee shop just to get out of the house, often wanting to visit with the other but both still harboring some embarrassment about their own lack of motivation, and both a little intimidated by the way in which the other was able to cast certain things into the light.

And so, life went on, as it does.

Early in the spring, after the snows had melted but before the too-short Wisconsin spring weather arrived, Jan knocked on Leif's door to ask a favor.

Leif opened the door, still in sweatpants and a sweatshirt. The need for snow removal was long passed, and it was still a few weeks before he would pick up his job at the Blue Bird Restaurant again. Jan was in overalls and a sweater, and from the mud and dirt it appeared she had been doing yardwork. Leif could never see her at work, but little clues here and there suggested that she had stuck with her plans of bringing new life to her backyard.

"Hello, Leif. How's it going?"

"Oh, fine. Yourself?"

"Good. Good. Hey, I was wondering...I want to go to the high school's band concert tonight. Will you go with me?"

It took Leif a moment to process what she was asking. He hadn't thought of going to a band concert in years, and had not expected it to be something Jan would want to do. He also wasn't sure why Jan would want him to go with her, except for the fact that he wasn't sure she had made any other connections since moving into town at the end of the summer.

"Um, I guess I could do that. I'm not doing anything else. You're just...interested in hearing some live music?"

"Yeah, live music. Who doesn't like that? It's been too long since I've been to a concert."

He knew she wasn't being truthful.

"I enjoy live music, although I have to admit high school band concerts aren't what I usually have in mind. But okay. What time is it at?"

"Six."

"And who's driving?"

Jan shrugged. "I can."

Leif and Jan sat near the back of the auditorium, waiting for the concert to begin. Leif had been surprised to realize it was the first time he had been back inside his old high school since he left for Afghanistan, and it stirred his memories in a mix of nostalgia and a relief that those days were behind him. Those times seemed a world away, and the person he was then seemed a stranger, but the kind of stranger he knew everything about, even if he failed to understand why that person acted the way they did. To an outside observer, high school would have been a great time for Leif, but he looked back at that person with slight embarrassment and regret, even if he couldn't help but feel wistful for the near-limitless optimism of the young man who was popular and well-liked, who earned high grades, made all-conference in basketball, and dreamed of being an honest politician as he handed out fliers for George W. Bush and Mark Green.

As they waited, Leif looked around the auditorium for people he recognized and found a few. Some were parents of people he knew in high school, like Mr. and Mrs. Bergland, who still looked like a young couple, even though they had seemed so old to Leif when he was growing up. Zach, a classmate of his, was their oldest, and now ten years later they were still doing the things that parents of high schoolers do.

This got Leif to wondering about who in the band he might know – or at least which family names he might recognize. He had been distracted and not taken a program on their way in, but Jan had one and she was glancing through it.

"Hey, can I see that when you're done with it?"

Jan looked over at him and then hesitated.

"Oh, um…"

"Just whenever you're done looking at it. I want to look at names."

Jan opened her mouth to say something, then shook her head.

"Yes, yes of course, I'm, uh, I'm done with it now."

She handed him the program, though it seemed like she was surrendering it with reluctance. Leif took it and said nothing.

He glanced through the names and was surprised how many were unfamiliar to him, even if he could make educated guesses as to whom many of the children belonged. He continued to scan through names as the lights dimmed a little more and the underclassmen band filed onto the stage and into their chairs. The band director came out last and stepped to their music stand and the music began. Leif closed the program and gave his honest attention to the performers.

After the underclassmen band played and left and the upperclassmen began to file onto the stage, Jan tapped Leif on the arm.

"Could I have the program back?"

Leif nodded and handed it back over to her. He noticed that she gave it only a cursory glance before turning her attention back to the stage.

And then Leif noticed, amongst the predominately white students, a short, slender girl with jet black hair and lightly-bronzed skin, carrying a tenor saxophone that would have looked too large for her if she didn't seem so comfortable with it.

His mouth dropped open.

"Hey, could I actually look at something in there real quick once?"

Jan's head slowly turned towards him, and then they held eye contact for a long moment. He sensed that she knew. She nodded and handed the program back to him without saying anything. He opened it and looked at the woodwinds section for the upperclassmen band, and just as he was scanning names, Jan's hand appeared, her index finger tapping a name.

Lily Huang.

He turned towards her, not hiding his surprise.

Jan smiled.

"Enjoy the show. We'll talk after."

They ducked out of the auditorium as soon as the show ended. Jan seemed in a hurry to leave, and Leif was impatient for answers to questions. During the show, he had continued to look around the auditorium trying to find anyone who looked like they might also have the last name Huang, but couldn't see anyone.

After a brisk walk through the parking lot to Jan's car, Leif jumped right into asking questions as Jan started the car and began to head for home.

"Okay, so who is Lily Huang?"

"My niece."

"Your brother's daughter?"

"Yes."

Jan answered both questions after the slightest pauses and delivered each word with weight, like she was pacing herself for questions of increasing difficulty.

"And so both of her parents are…" Leif realized he was talking too quickly and needed to be sensitive and tasteful in his curiosity. "…they're both…"

"They're both dead, yes. Her mother when she was two and her father when she was five."

Jan's voice was steady. She continued to deliver her answers in a measured tone as she navigated the city streets towards the county highway. Leif was not so steady, his heart quickening as he learned more and asked more.

"I'm sorry to hear that," he said, a rote courtesy. "And so now who does she live with?"

"Her grandparents – my mother and father. They've lived here in Badger Creek for almost ten years now."

"I see." Leif wasn't sure of the next question to ask. Part of him felt he had learned enough, but now that he was starting to get more answers, he thought he might as well press on. Besides, he had been open with her about Afghanistan and they did have a pact. "Is this…have you seen her since you moved here? Have you seen your mom and dad?"

Jan shook her head. She hadn't looked over at him once since she started driving.

"I wanted to go to her swim meets, but I was afraid I might run into my parents. This seemed safer, with there being more people and dimmed lights. I was still nervous about it."

"Why is it like this? I mean, why don't you want to see your parents? And is this…is this why you moved here?" Leif could feel the questions start to tumble out of him. He wanted to know everything. He wanted to piece it all together and understand this mysterious lady who lived next door.

When she didn't answer right away, Leif looked over at her to see that tears were streaming down her cheeks, even though she wasn't making any crying sounds.

"Oh, Jan, I'm sorry, I…"

She took a deep, quivering breath, and sighed, still not breaking into sobs, even though the tears continued.

"It's fine, it's fine. I'll tell you. Why the hell not? You're the one person in this new world I really know and if not you then who?" She laughed a nervous laugh and blinked tears from her eyes. "I guess it's time I tell you a story."

Jan arrived at the junction that would take them towards home, but turned the other way. Apparently she would need more time to tell the tale.

"My brother Khoi and I grew up with our parents in Green Bay. We both went to college – me at Madison and he at Milwaukee – and both moved right back to Green Bay for work. Being nearby and getting a good job – or at least a job that made good money – made up for the fact that I was getting close to 30 and hadn't had a boyfriend since high school. But Khoi came back from college with a serious girlfriend, Pham, and everyone loved her and looked forward to the family they would raise together. My parents even got over the fact that she was Catholic, and they hate Catholicism because of Ngo Dinh Diem, but they can adapt when it suits them. Anyway, they soon had a daughter – Lily, and from the first moment I met her she came to dominate my world. I loved my brother and I loved Pham, and silly as it sounds I could tell that even as a baby, Lily had the best of both of them. I also knew that I was probably never going to have a child of my own.

"Like I said, Pham died when Lily was two, killed by a drunken driver as we drove home from a ski trip. And from that day I started to be like a mother to Lily. I doubt she even has a single memory of Pham. And while our parents did a lot to look after Lily, I spent as much time as I could with her.

"Then, just three years later, Khoi was killed and Lily came under the full protection of her grandparents. And I began to be even more involved. I successfully arranged to work about half of my hours at home just so I could spend more time with her. My mother and father did a fine job raising me and my brother, but they have their…their ways of doing things, and they can be difficult, and they didn't always know when they wanted to assimilate into American culture and when they wanted to be Vietnamese, and I just thought it would be better for Lily if I was more the one who shaped her, even if they were – in truth – the ones who were raising her.

"But around this time I met a woman named Fiona through work. We got along so well and became friends before either of us knew that the other was interested in women. Once we learned that about each other, our relationship turned romantic. We were both each other's first true loves, and we were each the first person the other came out to. It was so fun and exciting and the risk in it – most people, including our families, were still pretty homophobic – it was another world, another world that we were the only ones in. And I thought, as much as I missed Pham and Khoi every day, I had Fiona and I had Lily, and that was enough. I didn't need anyone or anything else.

"And then my parents found out about Fiona. I guess these things can't stay secret forever, and eventually they would have known if we had ever moved in together, but their finding out while it was still secret could have only made it worse. And it was terrible. They were furious with me, and almost instantly wanted nothing to do with me. Buddhism doesn't prohibit homosexuality, but I think this was part of their drive to assimilate into American culture. They couldn't make the respectable American family they envisioned with a lesbian daughter, I guess.

"It hurt, losing my relationship with my parents, of course. But worse still, they gave me an ultimatum: have nothing to do with Fiona, or have nothing to do with Lily. I had to make a choice, what seemed an impossible choice, between my lover and my niece. Between one half of my world and the other.

"I couldn't bear to say goodbye to either one, so I thought I would try to keep them both. I decided I would tell my parents that I wouldn't be gay anymore, and that I had broken up with Fiona, so that I could continue to be with Lily.

"It didn't work. And I should have known it wouldn't. I told Fiona what happened, and I told her it would be years before we could live together or – if the laws changed – get married, and that we would have to go on in secret. And it broke her heart. To her, it was a rejection, a withholding, and she eventually ended everything between us. And when I went to try to claim my place by Lily and to salvage my relationship with her, my parents could tell I was not sincere. The heartbreak was written on my face, and my words rang hollow, and they feared I would love another woman and taint my young niece. And so they forbid me from ever seeing her again. So I lost them both.

"I've thought back on what happened a million times, trying to decide if there was something I could have done to hold onto one of them, let alone both of them, and I still don't know if I was doomed from the start. I think maybe I was. But here I am – screaming at my father about trying to send gifts to my niece, with no idea where in the world Fiona is, sneaking into band concerts just to see Lily for a few moments. And telling this strange young man everything as I gradually wend my way back to our homes in the middle of nowhere on an otherwise unremarkable, cold, dark spring evening."

Leif did not speak for a long time. When he did, all he could manage, in a soft voice, was to say, "I'm so sorry." Jan did not reply. He continued. "Thank you for telling me. And…I hope it helped you to say it. If it didn't, then I'm sorry for that too. I can't even imagine what that's like for you. And I just want you to know…" He put his hand gently on her shoulder. "I just want you to know that I'm here for you, in whatever way I can be."

Jan finally looked over to him as she turned onto their road. She smiled briefly.

"Thank you, Leif," she whispered.

They did not talk again until Jan pulled into her driveway and they got out of the car. Perhaps against his better judgement, Leif hazarded one last question.

"Jan, how did your brother die?"

She avoided looking at him for a moment, then stared straight at him across the top of her car.

"He was murdered. While hunting. By hunters. You know his name and you have the internet. You'll find any more that you're looking for there."

She turned away and strode towards her house.

Leif's mouth dropped and he hurried after her, shocked and embarrassed.

"Jan, wait, I'm sorry," he said, reaching out for her.

She whirled around and threw her arms around his body, burying her head in his chest, weeping. He gently laid his arms around her shoulders and held her there. They stayed like that for a long time as the flames of memory burned away the fog that shrouded the way forward, the way towards something new and different, if not always better or brighter.

Seventeen: In the Summer

Lily walked along the rows of knee-high corn in Mr. Leonardson's field towards the tree stand. It was a hot, humid day, and she looked forward to going to the Y later to swim some laps in the cold pool. Uncomfortable as it was outside, she had the day off and decided it was a good opportunity to go out to her hunting grounds and have a look around, just to see if there was anything interesting or out of order. She was not the kind of hunter satisfied with the bare minimum, never scouting her land or maintaining her equipment or cleaning and sighting in her rifle. For her, hunting was a year-round activity, one which could culminate in a moment of sudden violence, but one which was composed mainly of a long series of tasks. She hadn't visited Mr. Leonardson's land since she came out for the spring turkey hunt, and, with the bow hunt fast-approaching, it was past time she walked the grounds and inspected the stand.

On hot days like this one, Lily was wont to complain, but she remembered that her grandparents had grown up, worked, and fought in a land even hotter and more humid. Sometimes she felt like her grandparents were so out of touch and didn't understand at all what it was like to be an American teen, but so often she found her own challenges paled in comparison to what they had faced as rebels, revolutionaries, and immigrants. They would laugh at heat like this, even in their old age.

She wondered if Aunt Hoa had gotten used to the heat in Vietnam after moving there. It made her sad to think about her aunt who she loved and missed, and she still didn't understand why she only called once or twice a year and why she never came to visit. Someday, Lily would make a trip to her grandparents' home and then she would see her aunt again.

Even though the heat boiled her brain, Lily enjoyed the time to walk outside and let go of the mounting stress she was starting to feel as the beginning of her senior year approached. She was going to have a heavy course load, and she had decided to remain involved in band, track, and swimming for this final year. She had a real shot at winning a gold medal at state swimming this year, and it would make all those hours at the pool really seem worth it. She was also facing a decision about college, which could only come after she applied and got accepted. Her grades and test scores and extra-curriculars were good, but she was still afraid of not getting into all the schools she wanted. And, if she did, she didn't know how she was going to decide between the likes of Berkley and Johns Hopkins. Somewhere in the middle of all this, she hoped to be a teenager, if only for a few moments here and there.

All these things were filed away for later when she walked out into the fields and forests, drowned out by the cicadas and the meadowlarks and the steady presence of the trees. This time in the countryside was a time of peace when she could focus on one thing that was a part of everything.

She reached her stand and started to examine it. She checked the supports to make sure there was no rot in the wood and nothing giving way in the earth underneath. She tested the ladder's integrity and climbed up towards the box. She always hated going into the stand in weather like this, when she could hear flies buzzing and knew there had to be bugs and spiders, and maybe even a hornet's nest. She had meant to spray the stand with some repellent, but had not gotten around to it with her busy schedule. It didn't much matter to her since it was cold enough by the time she started using it that the unwanted visitors would be gone.

She opened the door with care, and breathed a sigh of relief when she was not greeted by anything larger than flies. Everything looked in order in the stand, although the windows could have used some cleaning. Satisfied, and relieved that she would not have to undertake any major projects, she climbed down from the stand and began looking around to see if she might find any game trails.

At the edge of the woods 30 yards from the stand, she found what looked like a worn path. The undergrowth was trampled, and some small branches had been broken away. She had killed a deer that emerged from this spot two years ago, and by the looks of things deer were still using it to enter Mr. Leonardson's field in order to cross it and head towards the next property. She imagined how the route must go when the path left the forest and traversed the field, and she traced the route with her eyes towards the other side of the field.

As she did so, she spotted a man walking from the other side of the field towards her. He was still a hundred yards away, walking right through the rows of corn. It wasn't Mr. Leonardson, so Lily didn't know who it was, and this made her nervous. In fact, her heart began to race the moment she processed that the man was walking right towards her.

She didn't know if she should call out to him, or hurry away, or just wait for him to arrive. Perhaps it was a neighbor out looking for their runaway dog. Maybe that was all it was.

The man got closer. He looked to be in his forties, of the average build complete with a developing beer belly, wearing jeans despite the heat and a dirty t-shirt and ball cap with the bill bent small. He was close enough now that she could tell he was looking at her, but he seemed unmoved by her presence. He just continued to saunter across the field, not looking at or for anything in particular.

Lily's heart continued to race and she felt the urge to walk quickly back towards the farm, but she felt frozen to the spot, like it might cause her trouble if she made any sudden movements. She tried to not think about what her father felt like in those final moments in a field somewhere in Casco.

The man stepped out of the rows of corn, now just ten feet away from her, and then he stopped on a dime and looked directly at her. His expression was blank.

"H…hi," Lily managed to rasp.

"Hey, Girl Scout," said the man. His voice was languid and suggested condescension. "Catching butterflies?"

Lily had no idea what to do with that. She was trying to come up with a serious response, not processing that the man was making fun of her. There seemed no reason for him to regard her like that.

The man laughed and shook his head. "Always saying, always saying," he said, although it was not clear what he was saying. "Think you should go home now."

Lily hated the way he laughed. A slight grin had crept onto his face, and she hated that too. She still couldn't say anything. None of this made any sense.

"You speak English?"

Lily snapped to reality. "Yes, I speak English. I speak lots of English. And I'm not a Girl Scout, I'm a hunter. That's my stand over there." She gestured towards her stand. Her voice shook a little but she met his unnerving gaze. Then she pressed the offensive. "Who are you and what are you doing here?"

The man kept his grin. "Out for a walk. Looking around. Thought I might find something to…see."

The pause he made sent a chill through Lily. He seemed to be acting creepy on purpose now. She didn't know if that was worse than him being this creepy without realizing. She wanted to ask him if he was lost or tell him to get lost, but her nerves had deserted her.

"Oh, nice day for that I guess. But I'm just headed in now. So, bye."

She started to walk away. She couldn't hear if the man had gone on either. She didn't want to look back, but she had barely started away when she did. He hadn't moved. He was watching her go.

"What's your name? I'll let Mr. Leonardson know that you're out here, since I assume you have his permission." She managed to make this sound innocent enough, even though she meant it as a threat.

She thought she could see a brief wave of uncertainty wash across the man's face. "Oh he knows me. Don't need to bother him. I'm just passing through." Without waiting for her to respond, he turned and left, disappearing into the woods, treading all over the deer path.

Lily had never walked as fast as she did back to the farm, breathing heavy, sweating and fighting back tears. The Leonardsons weren't home, but she would let herself into the cool air of the house and get a drink of water and try to calm down. Then she would call Mr. Leonardson and ask if he actually knew the man. She tried to reassure herself that he was just a man out looking for his dog who happened to be a little strange. He wouldn't be the first weirdo she had met.

She let herself in and was soothed at once by the respite from the heat and humidity. She went to the kitchen and poured herself a glass of water, draining it in one continuous series of gulps. She exhaled and took a few deep breaths. She looked out the window to make sure the man hadn't followed her, and she tried to slow her breathing even as she felt her heart continue to race. She opened her phone and called Mr. Leonardson's cell, hoping he'd pick up.

He did.

"Hello, this is John."

"Hi, Mr. Leonardson, it's Lily."

"Hi, Lily. You come out to the place yet?"

"Yes I'm here now. Everything looks good but there was a man."

"A man?"

"Yes there was a man walking across your field."

There was a pause. She could imagine a confused expression on his face.

"I…uhhh…I don't know who that'd be. Maybe one of my neighbors. Or, you know, you know what…I bet it was one of them roofers that's over there at Darrell's.

Yeah, there's been some guys working on the roof over there. Maybe he was just out walking around on a break or something."

Lily felt a little reassured, as the man looked like he could have been dressed for that, but she didn't know who would want to walk through fields and forests during their break from outdoor manual labor.

"Oh, okay. Yeah, maybe that's what it was."

"Did you talk to him?"

"No," she lied. "I could just see him as I was walking out there. You're probably right. He looked like he could be a roofer."

"Yeah. Probably. Well, thanks for looking out for the place and letting me know. Was that all you wanted to call about?"

"Yes, that's all."

"Okay, well, if you're leaving now I won't see you, but I'll see ya around."

"Yeah, I'll see you later."

They said goodbye and she ended the call. She refilled her water and took another long drink. Maybe the man was just a roofer, but she only felt a little better.

She decided it was time to go for a swim. Some vigorous laps would take her mind off things.

Eighteen: Waiting

Summer was good for Leif and for Jan. Jan spent more time outside and worked hard in her garden. The gardening and landscaping had her making frequent trips to the hardware store, seed store, farmer's market, and the co-op, and she steadily started making connections. She joined a book club and made a point to go to outdoor concerts and the touristy events which came one after the other during the summer months. She often invited Leif for lunch or dinner and she taught him how to make gỏi cuốn, though she held out on the chocolate cake recipe. She also, after asking Leif, hosted Jason, Liz, and Luke for dinner, and sent meals to Anders, Mindy, and baby Audrey.

Leif's time became more occupied and settled into a rhythm with work at the restaurant, and the momentum this gave him propelled him to spending less time inside his house and more of it out and about. Sometimes he would catch himself and wonder if his improved mood was just a case of being too busy to be bothered, like he was just staying a step ahead of depression and apathy on the treadmill of a busy schedule. Perhaps he would face the same kind of doldrums in the winter again, but that was a long way off, and there was so much between now and then, including everything that would come with autumn. So, whether he was ignoring issues or not, he was fine with the buoyancy provided by scooting from one table to the next during busy mealtime hours at the Blue Bird Restaurant.

While it wasn't quite like the weeks around Independence Day, late August remained busy, and Leif's shifts hummed along with a steady stream of people taking time for a nice, comforting meal on their vacations, along with the locals who didn't mind maneuvering through the busy downtown streets in the middle of the day.

Leif was in the rhythm, moving from table to table, attending to guests' needs, helping his junior coworkers, and winning over gratuities with smiles, decorum, and a well-timed joke here and there. He dropped off a check with a family of five and then weaved his way towards one of the larger booths to wait on a group who had just sat down.

He arrived at the table to find eight teenage girls.

"Hello," he said, smiling but careful not to seem flirty. That would do nobody any good. "My name's Leif, I'll be taking care of you guys today. We have a lunch special on quiche, if you're quiche people, and our soup of the day is potato and bacon. Can I get anyone anything to drink right away? We have iced coffee and tea for hot days like today."

The girls began to order drinks – though most of them just wanted water to start. Leif looked from one to the next and made marks on his notepad. He looked up from marking down another water and then he froze.

He was looking Lily Huang in the eye.

His heart skipped a beat and he didn't hear her say "Orange juice, please."

He recovered and pretended he hadn't quite heard her. He tapped his ear and said, "One more time?"

"Orange juice, please."

She smiled and it was a carbon copy of Jan's.

"Gotcha," he said, finishing the drink orders and heading back towards the kitchen by way of another one of his tables.

He continued to do his work, but he flipped on auto-pilot as his mind raced everywhere and nowhere at once. He had never thought much about what would happen if he happened to meet Lily, although he had scanned his memory files to see if he had ever encountered her before without knowing it.

Perhaps he could have written it off as a chance meeting with the friend of a friend – even if that didn't do the relationship justice – but he found himself so affected by this meeting, by this person in his presence, because from the first moment he felt compelled to tell her what he knew.

The thought had come to his mind unbidden and now he couldn't shake it or the notion that it was something he could do. He could find some way to tell this young person that her aunt who loved her so much was here in the same town as her, trying to keep tabs on her, hoping for a chance to reestablish a connection. That wasn't his place, of course, but it could be for the best. The friendship he had developed with Jan was built in large part on crossing lines, on pushing the envelope, and in fact their pact had begun after Leif made a literal intrusion. She wouldn't even have to know that he had done anything – Lily could find a subtle way to reconnect with her aunt without it being obvious that someone had told her. Besides, in a town this small, they were sure to run into each other at some point, especially now that Jan was spending more time out of the house.

He returned to the table of teenage girls with their drinks, and while he tried to act normal, he tried too hard not to stare at Lily even as he stole glances at her. If any of the other girls were watching him, they might have picked up on his unusual behavior.

"Do we need a few more minutes to look over the menu?"

The girls exchanged glances and giggled and shrugged until Lily took charge and spoke for them.

"Yes, at least a few. We've hardly looked at it," she said, her expression suggesting to Leif a mutual understanding of the peculiar way groups of teenagers order food.

"Sure, I'll be back around."

It was absurd for him to think that he could find some way to tell her that would not be some combination of awkward and inappropriate. Slipping her a note on a napkin was too risky, and there was no way to tell just her and not the other girls at the table, unless he just dropped it into conversation. But then that would take explaining and make for an uncomfortable situation.

But the situation was already uncomfortable. Leif had found himself a part of this story, of this situation of hurt and loss that dominated so much of the life of his neighbor, of his friend. He couldn't just sit idly by, but perhaps barging into the action of the story, rather than just being a sympathetic observer, was not the way to go about trying to help Jan. On the one hand, it was none of his business. But, on the other hand, he was the only person in the world – so far as he knew – who could do something to try to bring Jan closer to her niece again.

The debate continued to play out in his mind for as long as Lily and her friends were at the restaurant. He continued to operate on auto-pilot with his coworkers and other tables, and each time he returned to the girls he knew he had to be giving off at least a little awkwardness. When carrying a tray of food to them, he heard Lily laugh just like Jan and he almost spilled everything, adjusting the tray as the plates started to slide towards the edge. He played it off for laughs, but he could feel the sweat on his brow.

And the girls were there for a long time, talking, laughing, and eating a large lunch. He picked up that they were all athletes in the midst of some of their most grueling summer workouts. When he asked for dessert, there was that same deference and giggling as at the beginning of the meal, but this time they all at once turned to him and said *Yeahhh*. The Blue Bird did have some excellent desserts, and Leif never judged anyone who tacked on an overpriced finale to their already pricey meal.

He took their orders of cakes, brownies, and custards. When he turned to Lily she was still looking at her menu with indecision. She looked up and asked, "Is the chocolate cake good?"

Leif responded without thinking. "It is, although there's no special secret ingredient."

He met her gaze as he said this, and the slightest confused expression danced across her face for just a moment. "Oh, but it *is* good? I mean, it's still got chocolate, right?"

"Y-yeah," said Leif. "It's definitely got that."

"Well then I'll have that, even if it doesn't have a secret ingredient."

The next girl also looked confused before she ordered, like she thought Leif and Lily were riffing on an inside joke or secret knowledge.

He finished taking the orders and left the table. He wondered if she had picked up on what he was saying, but it seemed unlikely. It had been something extra that he said, certainly, but it was not so conspicuous or particular to convey to a young woman that he knew her long lost aunt and had tasted her grandmother's secret recipe chocolate cake. That was too much of a reach. Surely Lily's confused expression was just due to the superfluity of his comment.

But there was still something in that look, something unspoken that passed between them in a flash, some recognition of something that not just anyone could know.

By the time he returned with the desserts and confirmed that they wanted separate checks, Leif was just about settled on the debate. He still felt like he could tell her and that it might do some good, but he had punted on the decision long enough now that soon she would walk out the door and the opportunity to act would be gone, and he could think on it more outside of the heat of the moment.

He was just heading back to the table with the checks when he turned and almost ran into Lily, who looked to be on her way to the restroom.

"Ope," they both said.

"No you're fine," said Leif.

"The cake was good," said Lily, smiling. They weren't close enough to the restroom for their conversation to be awkward.

"Best you've ever had?" said Leif.

"Noooo, I've had better."

"I know you have."

Their gazes met again and now Leif was certain there was recognition in the confused look Lily returned, a look that simmered below a skeptical smile.

"You...know I –"

"Your aunt is my neighbor."

He blurted it out, not giving his inhibitions a chance to stop himself.

Lily blanched.

"You...what? My aunt? Do I know you?"

"No, but your aunt Hoa is my neighbor. I'm sorry, I don't know what you know."

"My...my aunt lives in Vietnam."

Leif's heart was racing. There was nothing for it now.

"You *are* Lily Huang, yeah?"

She nodded.

"Your aunt Hoa lives here. She goes by Jan. She just moved here about a year ago. We...we went to your band concert last spring and that's when I found out. Look, I...this probably wasn't for me to tell you. No, I know it wasn't. But I know you mean a lot to her and she means a lot to me and I just couldn't stand thinking of you not knowing that she's here and maybe if you know then somehow you can reconnect..." Lily wasn't responding other than a few slow nods. Her eyes were wide with shock. "I'm...I'm sorry – this is a lot."

"Um, yeah. Yeah it is. And now I have to find her. How can I do that? Can you tell me where I can meet her?"

"Oh, um, I...I don't want her to know that I told you. Maybe she'd be upset."

Lily squinted. She looked annoyed.

"No, I think you owe me this. Maybe I can keep that a secret, but you can't drop this at my feet and then leave me to solve the rest. Mister..." she looked at his name-tag, having forgotten what to call him, "Leif."

"Um, well...she always goes to the farmer's market on Saturdays. Maybe you could run into her."

"At the same time every Saturday?"

"Yeah she usually leaves about 11. I don't know how much she's aged since you've seen her, I would guess you'll recognize her."

Lily rolled her eyes. "Yeah, you think? Not exactly a lot of Vietnamese people in Badger Creek."

Her shock had morphed into annoyance, but Leif thought it must be covering the confusing rush of emotions this news had brought.

"I guess that's probably right."

There was an awkward pause.

"Well, good luck, I guess," said Leif, floundering for the right words.

"Yeah, guess so."

They walked past each other, both settling back into a confused haze of emotional adrenaline.

"Leif."

He stopped and turned.

"Yeah?"

"Thank you."

Nineteen: Dah Game

The second Monday of September was the first Monday Night Football game of the season, and the Packers were playing. Anders had bought some new tailgating toys and had received tickets from work, so he invited Leif, Jan, Jason, and Liz to pile into his truck and buzz down to Lambeau for the game.

Leif took the front seat, arguing that he was tallest and Jason could cozy up next to his wife in the ample space left by Jan's small frame. And, since it was his brother's vehicle, he felt a little ownership over the spot he had occupied on many excursions, even if Anders always traded up to a new model before Leif could lose spare change or French fries in it.

It had been over a week since the last farmer's market, and Jan had yet to mention to Leif whether or not she had met her niece. He hadn't had a full conversation with her since then, but he thought she would have said something if the reunion had occurred. It seemed unlikely that she would find an opportunity to say something on this day, but that did little to put the thought from Leif's mind.

"It's just gonna be weird seeing someone other than Brett out there," said Jason.

There was a collective *mmmm* of agreement.

"I know it's been talked about so much, but I just can't get over the way he left," said Anders.

"What do you mean?" said Leif.

"I just think when he decided to unretire that he should've come back and fought for the job and won it fair and square."

"You're gonna make the Hall of Famer compete for his job?" said Jason.

"Well, he left – it wasn't his job anymore. If he wanted it he should have proved it still belonged to him."

"I think he knew he wasn't going to be able to win it back," said Liz.

"What? Are you out of your mind?" said Jason.

"No, I think Aaron Rodgers is going to be really good. I think Brett and everyone knew it was time for a change."

There was a collective *ehhhh* of uncertainty.

"Well, he could've at least come back and given it an honest effort," said Anders. "If it was clear he wasn't good enough, I'm sure the team would've traded him to a situation where he could be happy. They would've done right by each other – but he had to make the first step."

"Oh I don't know," said Jan, smiling. "You millennials don't understand that we old-timers are used to being able to come back to the same job until we die or get bored. And we're just cranky in general."

Liz laughed. "The crazy thing is that he actually isn't *that* much younger than you. And he's still trying to play football!"

Jan waved her hand. "Bah, I'm old enough to be his mother." Then she looked up at the roof of the car, doing some quick mental math. "Er, wait…oh God, I really could be."

"You're not actually that old, though, are you? You don't look old enough to be *my* mother, let alone Brett Favre's," said Liz.

"Oh you. Yes, yes I am. But I like your reality better. Let's pretend I'm whatever age you think I am."

Leif had always felt like Jan existed outside of time, like her age didn't matter because it couldn't describe her. Sometimes he thought she was a friend from college and other times she seemed closer to a hundred.

"I definitely skew the average age in this truck, especially since I'm assuming I'm the one who took Luke's spot?"

"Maybe if it was a Sunday noon game," said Liz.

"It's too late on a school night," said Jason. "And the fans on Monday nights can be a little…well, drunk, for an eight-year-old. He's bummed, but we'll make it up to him."

Jan nodded. "Speaking of being the parent of a star quarterback, that guy's got a good arm there. When we played catch in the yard a few weeks ago I was really impressed."

"Yeah, he does have a pretty natural way of throwing," said Jason.

"I hope he wants to play when he gets older, but some of the things we're starting to hear about concussions…I don't know," said Liz.

"Yeah, I've been hearing about that," said Anders.

"Well, that's in professionals who have been playing for so long. Playing as a kid is different," said Jason.

Leif didn't contribute to this conversation, and became lost in thought about the balance of taking risks and playing it safe. He had been to war and never faced the risk of harm, and he wondered if now he should double down on that fortune and try something else that posed dangers physically or otherwise. Or maybe he should play it as safe as possible and preserve the time that hadn't been given to everyone who stepped out of a troop transport in Bagram. Maybe a young man should get the most out of life and play football and risk head injuries, knowing that they might just as easily develop pancreatic cancer. Or maybe they should try to preserve that cancer-free, war-free life and not take any risks, hoping no other unexpected obstacles stand in their way.

When there's a strange sound in the woods, sometimes the deer that runs off runs right into its death. And, sometimes, the one who stays put plays into the same demise.

The group enjoyed an early dinner of brats, kebabs, chips, cherry salsa, and a variety of cheeses in the parking lot of Lambeau. They all had a couple-two-tree brewskies as well, which fit right in with the sea of green and gold preparing to watch their team take on the Vikings with an afternoon's work of day drinking.

Leif felt good, which he did more and more as the beginning of autumn approached in earnest. Days like this one were the ones he looked forward to, and they were the ones when all things great and small could at least appear to dance in an orderly fashion. He was having a good time with his older brother and sister just being a Packer fan on a beautiful day. He was also happy to be around his friend and neighbor as she was enjoying herself, but even the sunshine and a Coors Light couldn't totally remove his uncertainty about what might have happened at the last farmer's market. He couldn't imagine Lily had not acted on his revelations, and if she had, he was certain Jan would say something, or reveal it in her demeanor. But she was just happy. Try as he might to be satisfied in that, he needed to know more.

Some of Anders' friends from work had joined their party. They were around his age and a mix of men and women, most of them the standard Wisconsin white collar model – good student from a small town, Madison-educated, successful at good honest work, starting families and continuing the cycle. One of them was talking about doing some campaign fundraising for John McCain over the weekend.

"It's a tough go trying to get anything done in Madison right now. The students love Obama. The younger demographic…that's going to be difficult."

"I don't know, McCain just doesn't get me all that excited," said Anders. "But I'm a Republican like you and I guess he's who we got."

"Something I don't like about Obama," said Jason.

"He's too young," said Liz.

"Too liberal," said another one of Anders' friends. "Someone more reasonable, well then maybe, I don't know. But not him."

"The young people just really do like him though," said the first man.

"Oh those *youths*," said Jan, smiling. "Don't you worry about them. If there's one thing old people like doing more than voting it's voting for other old people."

"You're in on McCain?" said Anders.

Jan laughed more loudly than she meant to. "Hell no."

"What about you Leif? You must support McCain, right?" said Jason.

Leif hadn't been paying much attention and was caught in the middle of snacking on some chips.

"Oh, uh, why's that?" he said, his mouth still full.

"Well, being a military man and all. You know he'll straighten out things in the Middle East."

Leif nodded as he swallowed his food.

"Uh, maybe. Maybe he will."

"Maybe?"

"Well, speaking as a military man, I'm telling you that there's more to fighting a war than fighting a war. And I'm also telling you there's more to being president than fighting a war. So, yeah. I haven't really thought about it much, but I don't know if McCain's right for the job. I don't know if Obama is either."

"You're a Nader guy?"

Leif rolled his eyes.

"Yeah, yeah I'm a Nader guy."

"Wait, seriously?"

"No, dummy," said Liz, elbowing her husband. "He's not a Nader guy."

As kickoff approached and the party started to think about packing up, Leif found himself hovering over the folding table of snacks, pilfering a few more before game time. He didn't feel like spending money on stadium food. He thought he was stealing a private moment as he scooped another chip full of salsa, and then he felt a presence at his side.

"Thought you'd get away with it, did you?"

He turned to see Jan reaching for a piece of string cheese.

"Wh-what?"

She gestured to the chips.

"Didn't think anyone would notice you trying to finish off all the leftovers?"

Leif laughed in nervous relief.

"Oh, yeah, darn, you caught me. There's just so much-"

"You told her, didn't you?"

Leif paused. Jan didn't look upset, but her face was serious.

Unable to find the right words, he just nodded and looked at their shoes.

"Leif. Leif, look at me."

He looked up and met her gaze.

"You gave away a secret that wasn't yours to give. You understand this, right?"

He nodded again.

"And you understand that I trust you, and that this wasn't very trustworthy, yes?"

Another nod, and he looked down again.

"Look at me."

He did.

"And because you did, because you did what I couldn't do…" she was choking up. "You brought my niece back into my life, and now everything is forever changed."

Leif half-smiled. "For the better?"

A tear rolled down her cheek.

"For the better."

She hugged him.

"Thank you, Leif. But don't ever be so sneaky again. That's not the way this works."

"I know. And I won't."

She stepped back from the hug and smiled, laughing at her tears.

"Okay, you clever man. Stop eating so we can clean this up and watch this game. I'm past ready for some football."

"Oh yah."

"Time for dah game, Leif. Time to watch dose Packers play dah game."

Twenty: Setting the Table

Leif and Lily looked over Jan's shoulder as she finished preparing their dinner.

"I told you, relax. Just go sit down and I'll finish up here," said Jan.

"There's nothing I-" said Leif.

"We," interjected Lily.

"*We* can do to help?"

"You can pour beverages. We're all having a beer," said Jan, turning down the burner on the pot of soup.

"I don't drink," said Lily.

Jan turned and looked at her, nonplussed. "Well. Of course you don't, and that's good. We'll have water then. You can get that and Leif you can…sing us a song."

"Wh-what?"

"I'm joking. I know you don't sing. Just relax and let me do this."

Soon they were seated, the food laid out before them, tall glasses of water poured and ready.

"Well, shall we pray?" said Jan. She noticed Lily look confused. "Oh, we always pray before our meals. Even though I'm a bad Buddhist and Leif is a bad Christian. But you're a good Catholic, so why don't you pray?"

"Oh…sure, I could do that, I guess. I don't usually pray out loud though."

"That's fine. Just pray in your head, but say the words out loud. And not one of those memorized prayers they do at Mass. An original one."

Lily still looked unsure, but eventually closed her eyes and folded her hands. Jan and Leif did the same.

"God…thank you for this meal – for the food and for the people I'm sharing it with. Thank you for your love and kindness and mercy. Help us be the same way. Um…yeah, amen."

Amen.

"Very good, if I do say so," said Jan.

"Apt," said Leif.

They began to pass the food – wild rice soup, sesame balls, cheese bread, and green beans – and eat.

"So, what I want to know," said Jan, "is which one of you is going to find this legendary deer everyone is still looking for?"

The two hunters laughed a little.

"Haven't seen it yet. Haven't had anything walk within range. Have you?" said Leif.

"I haven't either. I've seen lots of deer but they're all too far away. Honestly, I don't know what I'd do if I actually saw this deer, because just the sound of a deer running in the woods makes my heart just go crazy," said Lily.

"I know what you mean. Ever since I found out the deer was real, I haven't been able to get over this fever."

"And now *everyone* knows," said Jan. "Who's the dummy who leaked the photo online?"

Leif shook his head. "Who knows? But it's going to bring in hunters from all over for the gun hunt, I'm sure of it."

"Unless one of us gets it first," said Lily.

Leif smiled. "Right, unless one of us gets it first. It seems like *someone* has to. But, a deer doesn't live this long unless it's pretty clever."

"If the guy with the trail cam – Lenny, right? – if he had never told people about it, let alone gotten a picture, it's possible it'd still be his secret," said Jan.

"Makes you wonder why he told anyone," said Lily. "He hunts, right? He could've been the only one looking for it."

Leif laughed.

"You're right, but that's not the way of a man like that."

"What do you mean?" said Jan.

Leif took a bite of cheese bread covered in soup and pondered what he meant for a few moments as he chewed.

"This is really good."

"Thank you," said Jan.

"Yeah, it's all really good," said Lily. "Do you still make gỏi cuốn?"

"Oh yah," said Jan.

"Grandma makes it, but it's not as good as I remember yours being."

Jan smiled at her. There was a tinge of pain in it, but Lily didn't seem to notice.

"But, you were saying…" said Jan, turning to Leif.

"Right, right. I was saying…well, first, it's a small town, and secrets just don't get kept very well in small towns. People talk – about everything and nothing. I mean, you know this Lily, right? There's no secrets in your high school."

She shook her head. "Yeah, everyone knows everything. Although I surprise people sometimes."

"So there's that. But…the deer…for a man like Lenny, that deer is part of him, or what makes him himself. You, you're a young person who is a fan of things and has individual talents and interests and possibilities. Maybe sometimes it doesn't feel like it, since there's a lot of rules in your life, at school, at home. Probably one of the reasons you don't drink is that the law says you can't. But you do have a choice. And you get to calculate, and decide, and accept and reject. So you can keep a secret. You can choose what forms you, or at least try. A man like Lenny…he *is* his farm. He *is* this town. He *is* the woods and fields and the river. He's the people he's known all his life who have never been to Green Bay for any reason other than the Packers and Fleet Farm, and have never been further south than that. He doesn't separate himself from the world around him, and this place and everything that makes it what it is becomes his consciousness, becomes him. That deer was his secret but he could hardly keep a secret from himself. He shares the routines and cycles of his life with his world – he's certainly going to share perhaps the single most extraordinary thing that has walked into it. He had to say something. Otherwise…otherwise, it wouldn't exist."

Leif was staring off at nothing in particular, but Jan and Lily were staring at him, transfixed.

"The deer wouldn't exist?" said Jan.

Leif blinked and looked back at her. "Or any of it. None of it would exist…" his voice trailed off into a whisper.

There was a moment when no one spoke, unsure of how to transition. Leif continued by switching directions. "So! Lily, tell me about swimming."

The meal continued on, and they all enjoyed the food and conversation. The triad had only been brought together earlier that evening, but already they were all at ease with one another. Leif felt like he had known Lily a long time, and Lily understood what it was her aunt found in the young man.

"Well, I think it's time for dessert," said Jan, getting up from the table.

Leif smiled at Lily. "I wonder what this could be."

Lily looked confused for a moment, but then she opened her mouth in a silent *ah*. Jan returned a few moments later with three plates, each with a huge piece of chocolate cake.

"Somehow I think we all knew this would happen, didn't we?" said Jan.

"I think we did," said Leif. Lily was beaming at him. "Thank you for sharing this part of your world with me. I'm glad we all know this exists."

Twenty-One: Satisfactory

Leif hiked back across the soybean field from the woods to his house, frustrated. It was still early on a Sunday morning, but he had been out for a few hours and had seen nothing, and it was colder than he had expected. The rising sun and turning leaves were beautiful, but they did not match his mood. Since bringing down a doe a couple weeks earlier, he had been spending as much time as he could in the woods, certain that the bow hunt was his best chance at taking The Thirty Pointer before an army in blaze orange took up arms in late November. And still he had seen nothing of this animal.

Autumn was racing by again, and his hours at the restaurant were coming to a close. Finding this deer was climbing the list of his priorities and held powerful sway over his idle and active thoughts. But no matter how much time he put in, no matter how many early mornings he devoted, he had yet to be rewarded.

On this morning, he didn't feel like giving any more time to it. The peace granted by hours spent in the woods escaped him, and he decided to seek some satisfaction somewhere else.

It felt good to walk. Sometimes he wished the hike from Jan's woods to his house was a little longer. Walking somewhere with purpose was fulfilling, and there were peculiar charms to the comforts of a cool autumn day as well as the bracing, robust trudges through the snow. As it was, the walk was barely long enough to get lost in thought.

As he removed his boots and cold weather gear back in the house, he thought about what he might want to do instead, now that his schedule for the rest of the day was free and he had no intention of going back out into the woods until tomorrow. The Packers didn't play until late afternoon. He checked his watch and found that it wasn't even eight. He realized that most people his age didn't wear watches anymore, now that everyone had a cell phone. But he always had to wear one in Afghanistan, and he found he couldn't go into the woods without it, even if he sometimes resented being bound by hours and minutes and seconds.

He walked into the kitchen for a glass of water and to make some oatmeal. The sun was coming through the back window and the house was very quiet except for the creak of the floorboards as he walked.

As he fixed up the oatmeal just the way he liked it, with just a little milk, cinnamon, and peanut butter, he found himself wishing he had more opportunities to prepare food for others, the way Jan and his mother loved so much to do. In the stillness of a morning, there was something comforting about making a small meal all about himself and his satisfaction, but there was something about putting in that work for someone else, to meet someone else's desires, to serve and to share. He didn't know who this person was in his mind – a lover, a child, a friend, a stranger in need – but for a moment he almost felt like they were there with him, like he should set out another bowl and ask them how they liked their oatmeal.

And then he knew what he was going to do. He was going to go to church.

The thought was unexpected, but when it arrived there was almost no internal debate. He just knew that he was going. Surprised by his own immediate acceptance, he realized he didn't even want to go, but that it just felt right, like the thing he needed that was tailored just to how he was feeling then, like how sometimes he had no desire to go for a run but knew that it was the thing that would satisfy him.

Leif parked down the street from the Lutheran church he had grown up in, where his parents, his Grandpa (who was, remarkably, still alive) his aunt and uncle, and his sister's family still went every Sunday. Anders went to the non-denominational church where Mindy's family attended.

He parked far knowing that the church had many senior citizens. His father had always done the same thing, and had taught Leif it was the thing to do, especially since the church had such a small parking lot. As he got out of the car, he noticed his father's truck parked on the other side of the street. He smiled. Even if his father was old enough to warrant a closer spot, he was still taking the walk upon himself. And, if he knew his father, he would be letting his mother off just outside the door so she didn't have to.

He crossed the parking lot towards the door, crunching leaves underneath his feet. An elderly couple was ahead of him, the man hunched over a walker. He hurried to pass them and get the door. He got there well before them, and after opening the door right away, he realized he would be letting in a lot of cold air if he kept it open until they passed through. He shut the door and continued to wait.

"Oh, keep it open please," said the woman, seeming to just notice Leif.

"I will – just keeping the cold out," said Leif, biting back an annoyed response. He smiled.

The man looked up, which required him to stop moving forward. He unveiled a grin and whispered something that might have been *hi, young man.* Leif nodded. "Good morning."

That was what someone was supposed to say at church, he remembered. *Good morning.* It was so natural to him. *Good morning.* One might say that anywhere else in the morning – at work, at school, at Kwik Trip – but there was something extra mixed in when it was said at church. *Good morning. This is the day that the Lord has made. Let us rejoice and be glad in it.* Church words had stayed with him wherever he went. He didn't know if that made them sacred or kitsch. If they were as true as they were tried.

The couple finally passed through the door. Leif looked up from them to see that someone else was close behind.

"Hey there Leif!"

It was Mrs. Szynski.

"Oh, good morning, Mrs. Szynski."

She shuffled up to him, not passing through the door, and he had to keep it open.

"Haven't seen you in a while," she said. There was no accusation, just observation. He thought she might have tried to hug him if he hadn't been holding the door.

"Yeah, been a while." He didn't know what else to say other than that. Some feelings didn't have the right church words.

Mrs. Szynski smiled big. "Well it's good to see yah." She nodded to him and continued on into the church.

A younger couple were herding their young children across the parking lot towards the door, but Leif decided they were far enough away that he could finally let the door close.

Leif maneuvered his way through people milling about between the coat racks, bathroom, and sanctuary, and at almost every step he was met by a smile or a *Good Morning.* He recognized everyone, and everyone recognized him. Over the years of visiting church while home from college or on leave from the military or after his discharge, he had become adept at expediting church conversation. Church people always wanted to know what was going on in his life – or at least they asked those kinds of questions – and as a matter of necessity he had learned how to give concise, closed answers and transition out of the conversation. If he didn't, he'd exhaust himself trying to fully engage with every person who smiled and said hello.

The ushers greeted him with a firm handshake and a bulletin. When he arrived at the door of the small sanctuary, he scanned the pews for his family, looking to see if they were in their traditional place. They were, and he made his way over to sit next to them. The seats were beginning to fill up, though as he remembered it was rarely more than three-quarters full. The organist was playing a familiar hymn, "Children of the Heavenly Father.”

He arrived at the end of the row where his family was. His father was on the end of their group, and he didn't notice Leif until he began to shuffle his way into the pew. He looked up and his face lit up in surprise.

“Leif, you're…you're here.”

Leif sat down next to him and exhaled.

“Yeah, I'm as surprised as you.”

The rest of the family had noticed him by now and leaned to look towards him. It was a strange sort of unexpected meeting, as he spent plenty of time with his family, so it was not a long-lost prodigal son situation, but he had been absent from this context for so long that it was like being reintroduced to something already familiar.

Leif tried to act like nothing was out of place, paging through his bulletin. His father continued to look at him.

“What made you decide to come?”

Leif shrugged. “I can't honestly say I had anything better to do this morning.”

Clint didn't love that answer, and he frowned, but then it shifted into a slight smile. “Well, you're here. As you should be.”

Leif nodded and pretended to read the bulletin again. Then he realized someone was missing.

“Hey, where's Grandpa?”

“In the foyer. In case he needs the bathroom, then he's closer. And if he has a coughing fit, it's less disruptive.”

Leif turned towards the foyer to look for his grandpa, but more people were filing into the sanctuary and he couldn't see through them. He wondered how he had missed him.

“No one is sitting back there with him?”

“No,” said Clint, “he doesn't want to make anyone else do that for his sake. We try to, but you know how he is.”

Leif rolled his eyes towards his father. “Oh, I know, and I *know* you know. You are his son.”

“And you're mine,” said Clint, without missing a beat.

Leif shrugged. “Fair enough.”

As soon as the service began, Leif found himself daydreaming. It was a familiar problem for him. When he didn't feel like singing along with the hymns, he disengaged from the worship experience, and unfunny jokes during the announcements and an uninspired sermon did nothing to draw him back in. It frustrated him, because he thought he would like going more if he could feel like he was really there, but once his mind started to freely wander, it didn't seem worth it to fight to stay present. And so he spent the service thinking about the Packers, and Jan and Lily, and Afghanistan, and – eventually and inevitably – The Thirty Pointer. Even though he had had enough of the hunt that morning, he couldn't shake the idea of the time he had surrendered, and the possibility that the creature was walking through the woods right now, stepping into his shooting lane, presenting a broadside within range, giving him the opportunity to take it down with one well-placed arrow to the heart.

He had replayed scenarios like this in his mind thousands of times. It seemed so attainable, and if he did manage to do it, it would be one of the greatest highlights of his life. It would be something for him to hold onto forever. He would be in a rare class of hunters to ever accomplish something like it. He had to continue to think about it. It made it real.

Before he knew it, the service was over, and he once again engaged in successive small talks. And, as it turned out, more than one of these conversations brought up The Thirty Pointer. By now, with the creature's existence common knowledge, many people knew that Leif's hunting ground was one of the closest to the only confirmed sightings. And, with many people knowing that Leif was a deadly marksman, there was a certain amount of expectation that he would be the one to earn the trophy. This had become familiar to him, but it surprised him when this variety of conversation held sway even during post-service coffee time.

He was engaged in one such conversation when Liz appeared by his side, looking like she had something to say. The middle-aged man he was speaking to took the hint, and they wrapped up the conversation with another handshake and a smile.

"Hey, what's up?" said Leif.

"We're headed to lunch at Bailey's. You're coming, right?"

It was their favorite place to go for lunch on the Sundays when his mother didn't prepare a dinner. He wondered if this choice was a ploy intended to keep him around, but he wasn't about to say no.

"Heck yeah. We're leaving now?"

"Yeah, we'll meet you there."

"Great." He turned to go.

"Hey," said Liz, grabbing his arm. "I'm glad you were here today. Are you glad you were here today?"

He hesitated. "Yeah. I am."

She raised an eyebrow. "But?"

He shrugged. "No, you know what, I am. I really am. It was…maybe not exactly what I had hoped for but, it was good for me to be there."

Liz stared at him, and he knew his sister well enough to know she wasn't totally convinced. But he wasn't totally convinced either, so they understood each other.

"It doesn't have to knock your socks off every time," she said.

"That's right. It doesn't. And it didn't. But I didn't totally hate it."

She shrugged. "Well, I know you made Mom and Dad happy. Grandpa, too. And that's worth a lot."

"That *is* worth a lot. Think they'll pay for my lunch?"

She rolled her eyes and nudged him towards the door. "I guess you can hope so."

Twenty-Two: The Reaping

Jan's back yard yielded a bountiful harvest in both the summer and fall. Her vision for bringing an abundance of life into her small part of the world bloomed into flowers and grew up into a cornucopia of fruits and vegetables. It was more than she felt she could use herself, and she was happy to share as much of it as she could. Leif was keen to get some of the broccoli, turnips, Brussels sprouts, and basil.

"Of course," Jan had said, "just come on over whenever and I'll put some together for you."

And so on a cold afternoon when he wasn't doing anything else, Leif walked over to Jan's house to pick up his produce.

He rang the doorbell and waited. The wind added some bite to the cold November weather, and he shivered in his sweatshirt. Fall was racing past too quickly again, with winter whispering its approach in the frost of the mornings, the chill of the afternoon, and the depth of night. But still the amber and gold of autumn colored the air, and it helped that enough homes and businesses in Badger Creek resisted shifting into Christmas until at least Black Friday. Christmas shopping would be different this year with the way the economy had turned in September. Barack Obama had just been elected, and half the people Leif knew thought he would fix the problem in his first 100 days, and the other half seemed to think the country was headed for collapse.

He continued to wait, and Jan still did not come to the door. He had no way to know if her car was in the garage, but some lights were on – not that that meant much. Perhaps he should have texted ahead of time.

He rang the doorbell again and waited. It was late enough in the afternoon that he couldn't think of a reason why she would be out and about. Jan had her habits and routines, and by now Leif was familiar with them.

He thought he would invite Jan over for Thanksgiving again. It had been an enjoyable time last year, and she had developed a good relationship with his sister's family. What he didn't know was whether he would invite Jan to invite Lily. That would require Jan to reveal something deeply personal to a host of new people, and it would make the secret status of the situation which Jan wanted to maintain that much more tenuous. But Leif wanted Jan to be with her family on Thanksgiving, and that meant being with Lily.

But don't ever be so sneaky again, Jan had said, *that's not the way this works.*

Leif would let Jan make that call. Even if his intrusion had worked out in the past, he knew it had been a breach of trust. Jan would handle the situation the way she felt was best, and Leif had to trust that.

Jan still didn't come to the door. Leif tested the door handle and found it unlocked. She must be home – Jan always kept her doors locked when she was out of the house. In fact, she usually kept it locked when she was home, too. He eased the door open a little and stepped one foot in.

"Jan?"

He hoped she wasn't in the bathroom.

There was no response. It occurred to him that she may have been in the backyard. They had both quit smoking over the summer, but it was getting close to the same time when they had given into the old habit last year – maybe she was just taking a smoke break.

He made his way into the house and called out again, but there was no answer. He could have left then, but as long as he was already here he thought he'd just go out the back door and see if she was there. She'd probably be out there and would be happy to see him and would make a joke about him being an intruder.

Her house, like his, had a sliding door just off the kitchen that led to the back yard. He made his way into the kitchen and went to look out the glass door, which further suggested she was home as the blinds had been drawn back.

And as he looked out, his hand froze on its way to the door, and the world spun around him as a shockwave shot through his senses. It was like in basic training when he had been too close to a comrade on the firing range and his ears rang and he could hear his breath inside his head.

The Thirty Pointer was in Jan's backyard.

It was unmistakable. He had never seen a deer so large or a set of antlers so kingly.

And Jan was in the backyard too, feeding The Thirty Pointer out of the palm of her hand.

He blinked. And blinked again. And still he was seeing what could have only been a dream until it stood before him. Jan was holding out her hand like it was the most normal thing in the world, and the huge creature bent its head to take in what she offered, also seeming at ease, like it knew it was safe in the enclave of the yard.

Like this had happened before. Many times.

Leif could not have said how long he stood there, immobilized. He wanted to step out into the yard and bring this moment into reality, but he was afraid the sound of the door would send the deer running. He also had half a mind to run back to his house, get his bow and arrow and kill it then and there.

He needed to know what would happen next, and he bore the weight of setting the next moment into motion.

His hand came to rest on the door handle, and he eased the door open. At the sound of it, the Thirty Pointer appeared to stop eating for just a moment to listen.

Leif stepped out onto the deck, and then the deer raised its head and looked right at him. Jan did too, but Leif was not seeing her.

Leif and the Thirty Pointer stared at one another for a long moment, the man awed and terrified, the deer calm and assured. When the man took another step forward, the deer turned and walked away, not bounding away like deer are supposed to. It was unhurried. When it reached the boundary of trees, it lowered its head and pushed its way through, passing out of sight, and maybe, for Leif, into nothing but memory.

Leif released a breath, which he realized he had been holding. Now his eyes found Jan, who had been staring at him the entire time, not watching the deer leave. Now Leif advanced towards her with purposeful strides.

"You *knew?*"

"Leif, I…"

"It's been coming to your yard the whole time? You've been *feeding* it?"

"Just this year, I swear I- …"

He marched all the way right up to her, and she looked afraid, taking a defensive step back and holding up her hands.

"How could you do this Jan? How could you…"

He put his hands on his head, angry and in disbelief, unable to find any other words.

Jan was breathing heavy. She still looked scared, though she was composing herself. When she spoke, she did so slowly.

"I'm not going to apologize, if that's what you want. I feel bad about being deceptive, but not about not helping you find it."

"I thought you were okay with hunting? Lily's a big time hunter – she wants to kill it as much as I do!"

"I *am* okay with hunting. And with hunters. That doesn't mean I have to hand an animal over to you. If you found it in the woods, fine. But here, this is where my choices live. I get to decide what to do with a deer that wanders into my yard."

"It isn't your deer."

"No, and it isn't yours either. But you seem to think so – you and all the other hunters who can only think of its inevitable end. That it's *someone's* deer. That someone has to take it. I know you've never thought about hunting like that. I know Lily hasn't either. But this has been different. You know it has."

Leif was furious, and sputtered on finding a first word. "Fine, yes. Yes this is different. This is more than just a deer, this is…this was something I could get out of bed for. I knew it was close, I knew I could do it. I worked so hard. And you…you kept this from me."

Jan's face faded into sadness. "I told you I'm not going to apologize for that."

Leif shook his head and looked away from her. When he looked back, his face had softened too.

"You might be right in some ways. You usually are." He remembered the way she had stopped him from driving drunk last winter. "But you were still dishonest, or at least disingenuous. And…and I don't know what to do with that."

Jan shrugged. "I guess you might know something about that, wouldn't you?"

Leif knew he should just leave the yard and take some time to get over this offense before going further. But he decided to speak.

"This is about your brother, isn't it? This is about revenge."

Jan's eyes widened.

"How dare you. How dare you, Leif. You think I'm protecting a deer out of spite for the kinds of people who murdered Khoi? You think if I thought that could do something for me, or for my brother, or for his memory, that I would have ever let you hunt my land in the first place? That I would have invited you into my home? That I would let you near my niece? Do you really think that?"

Leif could feel the momentum of his mistake unravel a friendship before his eyes.

"I just thought that maybe…"

"You thought. You maybe. Leif, always blown about by the wind. Let me turn this to you then – is this about Afghanistan? Is this about sitting around uselessly and never taking a shot? You want to finally have a kill you can boast about? Want to have something to put your name on, give something to the legend of Hawkeyed Leif? One big deer to make up for all the-"

"Enough!"

Finally, they were both silent.

Only the wind made any sound, whistling through the trees and buffeting their ears which drummed with their racing, heavy hearts.

Leif whirled on his heel and strode towards the trees. Jan walked more slowly back to her house, tears already on her face.

And as they closed doors behind them, they faced their evenings in the wake of a pact that was as good as dead and buried.

Twenty-Three: Death Arrives

Grandpa Delmar died before Thanksgiving.

Coughing and wheezing, fading in and out of consciousness, murmuring this and that, it was a respite for Clint and Mary when he slept, and a relief when the doctors found them in the waiting room to tell them he had passed. Of course, neither of them said so. The end of life demands decorous behaviors.

The funeral was small and not quite somber. Most people of Delmar's generation had already passed, and those who knew him thought well of him. A few people showed up who had thought he had been dead for ten years.

It was Luke's first funeral. He understood death, but not loss, and he didn't cry. It was his cousin Audrey's first funeral, and she understood nothing, and would remember none of it either.

Their grandfather and Delmar's son, Clint, had been to more funerals than he could track. His first was his mother's, when he was eight. He had held his father's hand the entire time, terrified to let go. His fourth funeral was when his friend Mark killed himself with a drug overdose in high school. Mark's parents made it an elaborate affair to try to ease their pain. His fifth was when his cousin Lianne drowned in the summer of 1965. It was the largest, saddest funeral he had been to. His seventh was a hasty affair, a few words over the shattered body of Bucky Williams in a small village in the Quảng Trị province. It wasn't until he bore the flag-draped casket of Rodger Crane, who committed suicide in 1978, that Clint realized he had stopped counting.

He made a point to go to any and every funeral he could – so long as he had at least some connection to the deceased. Former comrades, distant relations, townies, church members, all of them. He never refused to be a part of the color guard in the annual Memorial Day ceremonies, nor would he decline to give a eulogy if asked – which he was, often.

He was silent and stone-faced through his father's funeral, until he gave the eulogy, when he focused on the best of Delmar, and he smiled and laughed through a funny story and allowed a tear when speaking of how his father had raised him after his mother died. Many people had been taken too soon from Clint, but his father was not one of them.

After the funeral service, the family began to go their separate ways. They had talked about getting together, but seeing as it was a Saturday they decided to wait until a customary Sunday gathering. Most everyone had plans for one of the last Saturdays that still felt like autumn, or, in the case of Anders and Mindy, a fussy one-year-old.

As his family and the other attendees left, Leif waited around the church and kept an eye on his father. He knew Clint had accepted for years that Delmar was not long for this world, and that it was not a bad way to see an old man go. Leif also knew that his father was not one for showing emotions. But there was a way in the manner his father stood in the church lobby, his shoulders hunched, his gaze drifting about, his jawline set, that indicated to Leif a pain beneath the surface of the man who shook hands and shared hugs and bid farewells to those who had come to see his father put to rest. With the rest of his family, besides his mother, having left, Leif felt it was on him to give his father an opportunity for further mourning.

The lobby was just about empty, and Leif approached his father, who was looking absently at a bulletin board of church announcements, his hands buried in his suit pants pockets.

"Hey, Dad."

His father turned to him in acknowledgement. "I…was wondering if you wanted to go to lunch with me."

Clint hesitated. Leif thought he might not feel like eating, but he was very hungry and he hoped his father would agree anyway.

"I thought we were just getting together tomorrow."

"Oh, the family is, yeah. I just mean you and me."

The words softened the set of his father's jaw and the furrow in his brow.

"Okay. Let me see what Mary thinks."

"No, I really meant just you and me. I mean, you spend all day with Mom. I thought we would go to Sully's. Like we used to with Grandpa."

Clint nodded slowly. "Okay, we can do that."

Leif wasn't sure how reluctant his father was, but he had agreed and that was enough, especially since he was so hungry.

"Okay. You can give your keys to Mom so she can get home, and I'll drive us there."

"You don't want to go home and change? We're in suits."

Leif waved his hand. "Home is the opposite direction. Let's just go." He started towards the door.

His father shrugged and followed, doing a cursory scan of the lobby to see if there were any last well-wishers who had condolences to offer.

"Would you rather sit in a booth or a table?" asked Leif as the hostess led them into the small dining room at Sully's Café.

Clint's eyes twinkled for just a moment as he recognized Leif was deferring to the needs of an aging man. "I can still get in and out of a booth," he said, turning to the hostess. "We'll take one of those if you've got a clean one."

They settled into the booth and ordered coffee when the waiter came to introduce herself and fill up their water glasses. They opened their menus and flipped through them, mostly just to make sure their old favorites were still there. Nostalgia held powerful sway on this day.

"It would be nice if Anders was here too," said Clint.

Leif nodded. "It would be. I'm sure he would have liked to, but little Audrey usually gets her way."

"Not that I mind it's just us," added Clint. "Really. This was nice of you."

"No, I know."

Leif took a moment to look away from the menu and gaze around the familiar dining room. There was no theme to the décor – in fact there was very little décor of any kind. Some of the few wall adornments were framed newspaper clippings about the restaurant. The café generated ambience through intimacy and breakfasts and lunches which achieved an uncommon blend of quality, quantity, and economy. And, on a cold November day, a clean, cozy, friendly space with a good meal would go a long way.

They said little as they waited for the waitress to return. When she arrived at the table with a carafe of coffee, Leif told her they were ready to order.

"BLT and broccoli cheese soup, please," said Clint.

"Sullyburger and fries for me," said Leif. There were other things on the menu he might prefer, but his grandfather had ordered him a Sullyburger with fries when he was seven and he had never strayed since.

The waitress headed off to the kitchen and they were alone again with their coffee, the steam rising lazily from the mugs.

Leif wasn't sure if he should go right for asking about how his father was feeling. Clint was quiet and didn't seem likely to ask questions to start conversation. He decided to go for a safe, albeit gloomy, conversation topic.

"Things aren't looking so good for the Packers, are they?"

Clint laughed a short, dismissive laugh and shook his head. "Two close losses and now they're below five hundred. Tough."

"They're going to have to win those kinds of games if they want to keep pace with Minnesota."

"Brett would've won those games."

Leif shrugged and smiled before taking a sip of coffee. "Yeah, he might've. But I like Rodgers. I think he's got a future."

"I've had enough talk of *change* as of late," said Clint, and Leif knew he was referring to Obama's campaign. They exchanged a look as Clint searched his son's eyes to see if he felt the same way about the president-elect, but neither one pursued the topic further.

They continued to talk football until their food arrived. Leif was about to pick up his burger when his father suggested they pray.

"Oh, of course. You want to?" said Leif.

Clint nodded and closed his eyes as they both bowed their heads slightly over the table.

"Lord, thank you for this meal – bless it unto our bodies, and thank you for the hands that prepared it. Thank you for this time for us to be together. And I pray we will remember and honor Grandpa Delmar. Amen."

Leif made his first act of remembrance for his grandfather by picking up the Sullyburger and taking a bite.

"It's been too long since I've had one of these," he said after chewing to his great satisfaction. "There were a few times when I was in Afghanistan that I just had such a craving for a Sullyburger." He winced internally. He didn't like to talk about his own military experience around his father. Or around anyone, but it so often found its way into conversation.

"I bet you did," said Clint.

Leif thought he would try to change the subject, but then Clint continued his thought.

"There were times in Vietnam when all I could think about was a cheeseburger, fries, and vanilla shake from McDonald's. Even in dangerous situations. It was absurd, you know? Life was hanging in the balance and suddenly I'm thinking about fast food." He picked up his soup spoon and brought it to the edge of the bowl, but kept talking before digging in. "I got my wish, eventually. When I got back – back for good, I mean – I ate so much McDonald's. It just…well I liked it, of course. And it was cheap. But I just felt like I was home when I was eating it. And it helped me know I wasn't going back…" he trailed off, and his spoon moved away from the bowl. "Do you know what I mean?"

Leif felt he could relate to so little of his father's war experience. There were shades and echoes of the same soldier's heart, but they were different realms of experience.

"Kinda, kinda," he said, chewing thoughtfully. "Well, but not exactly. But I can say that it does feel weird being here while it's still going on. Like, I *could* be there. And there are other people like me still there. But I'm not. And one time…" Leif ate a few fries before continuing his thought. While his father still hadn't touched his food, Leif hardly felt he could stop eating. "One time, I was making plans for something a few months out, and I thought to myself – *oh, I'm not going to be able to do this, my leave will be over by then and I'll be on deployment again* – and then I remembered that was over and done and I never had to go back. I still have dreams where I'm going back."

"And how do you feel when you wake up from those?"

"Terrified. Then relieved."

Clint nodded. He was listening intently to his son. "There's no shame in that, of course."

"I know," said Leif, still eating.

Clint didn't say anything more, and still held his soup spoon without using it. Leif realized his father was leaving the space for him to continue to talk.

"Well, anyway. It's in the past. I'm here and healthy and on to the next thing."

"Of course. And I suppose you just wear that scarf because it's so comfortable and fashionable?"

Leif paused mid-bite. "It *is* comfortable and fashionable."

Clint smiled. "I'm sure that it is. It's also a dead man's."

There was something to the way he said those two words – *dead man's*. They lilted together, his gruff voice flowing from one word to the next that left a haunting, cold weight on them that only someone who had known many dead men could ever deliver. It gave Leif a chill.

"Well, you...you keep reminders around too. Bumper stickers and stuff. And you do the honor guard."

"You're right, but I don't pretend those memories don't affect me every single day."

"Doesn't it...haunt you though?"

"Of course. Of course it does. Any reminder is liable to bring back a painful memory. I dream terrifying dreams, too."

"And you're able to remember it without dwelling on it?"

"I try, yes. I go forward. I can't choose what I bring with me – I don't think that's possible. That isn't up to me. The dead follow me just as the living surround me, and that changes how I live my life, but it doesn't stop me from living it. I just...well, I say a prayer, roll up my sleeves, and keep walking. That's how I made it through many patrols in Vietnam, and it's how I make it through whatever happens in small town Wisconsin. They're very different. But they have me in common, and that's quite a lot."

Leif had finally stopped eating, hanging on every word his father said. "And so... so while it hurts right now, and might hurt a month or a year from now, you're going to learn how to walk without your dad?"

Clint's brow furrowed and his eyes watered, but then he smiled. "Yes. That's what I'm going to do."

He finally put his spoon into his bowl of soup and began to eat – just as he would have if his father was there, too.

Twenty-Four: Ballistics

Lily Huang sped through the woods in her old pickup truck on the way home from an unsuccessful hunt. There were just a few days left in the gun hunt, and she had yet to find what she was looking for.

Darkness had set in. She had stayed out in her stand until the very last moment of legal shooting hours, and had still heard a couple of gunshots afterwards. Each one made her jump, and each one made her angry. Those shots were evidence of people being careless, of people not being safe. People died in the woods – usually by accident. She had heard that one person died in Outagamie County this season, and there had been some incidents of harassment and threats over hunting grounds.

When she learned that her aunt's land was so close to where the Thirty Pointer had been seen, she was worried that some people might trespass in her woods looking for it. And if they knew that the landowner was a tiny Asian lady that might make them bolder.

She put dark thoughts out of her mind and thought about Thanksgiving, which was the following day. She had asked her aunt if she would join her and her grandparents for dinner, but Jan had totally rejected the idea. Lily still didn't quite understand why her aunt and her grandparents had to continue to have nothing to do with each other. Of course there would be some tension, but she thought there was a way forward, and maybe a Thanksgiving together was the solution. She hoped that they could do away with the secrets eventually. She always found herself siding with her aunt, but she loved her grandparents too, and she didn't want to hide this from them.

Her aunt had mentioned to her that she had spent Thanksgiving with Leif and his family the year before, but she had not said anything about doing that this year. If she was, Lily wouldn't have minded joining them for at least part of the time. She liked Leif, and she owed her renewed relationship with her aunt to him. Maybe she would bring it up again with her aunt when she got home.

Her thoughts ran on and on as she raced through the trees and her headlights illuminated the old pavement and the faded yellow lines.

And then a gray blur flew across the road from left to right, making it most of the way before the truck slammed into it and sent it sprawling into the ditch. The percussive couple of seconds were over and done before Lily's world slowed to a crawl and it all replayed before her, slow enough on replay for her to recognize the phantom as a large deer dashing in front of her before the truck slammed into its flank mid stride, sending it flying and rolling away into the darkness.

She screamed, though she didn't realize it.

She slammed on her brakes and hunched breathless over the steering wheel. Then she turned the wheel and crept over to the side of the road. Her body was shaking, and she took a few moments to compose herself. She turned off the car and got out, her legs quivering as she stepped onto the pavement and opened the other door to retrieve her heavy duty flashlight from her hunting bag. She could hear something in the dead leaves and twigs in the dark back where she thought she had hit the deer.

She turned on the flashlight and walked with caution towards the sound. She had gone just a few steps when the lights caught the eyes of the deer, and then she could see a massive head and neck and then the huge body thrashing around on the ground. And then she gasped as she realized she had just hit The Thirty Pointer. She froze and watched, immobilized as the massive animal and its glorious set of antlers writhed in the ditch. Its legs must have been broken, and while she could not see any blood, she thought there must be some sort of internal damage from the blunt force trauma. She had been going at least 55, and it was not a glancing blow.

And she knew what she had to do.

She backed away and did not take her eyes off the animal until she got to her truck, afraid that if she lost sight of it the creature might disappear forever. She opened her truck again and retrieved her rifle. First she used some duct tape to fasten her flashlight to the barrel, and then she found her ammunition. As she loaded a magazine and chambered a round, she realized she was crying as well as trembling, but she had no doubt about what she was doing.

She turned back to the deer and approached it, walking more quickly this time, moving forward with purpose. She stopped about ten yards away – any closer seemed dangerous. It had not been able to get up, but she knew its flailing antlers and hooves could be fatal. It had managed to turn itself a little, and now it could see her. She didn't think it looked afraid – if deer could look afraid.

She wanted a quick and clean kill, but it wouldn't stop moving for her to be sure of a headshot. She would aim for the heart. Not any bigger a target, but if she missed, she would either miss entirely or hit the lungs, which was not bad. At least this way its regal crown would sit on an unbroken helm.

She clicked the scope back to its most basic magnification, then raised the butt to her shoulder and looked through the glass. She was still shaking, but a few deep breaths brought her just enough stability, and the crosshairs rested near enough where she knew that vital organ was.

She pulled the trigger and the night air cracked with the boom of the rifle. She lowered it as soon as she recovered from the recoil, the noise ringing in her unprotected ears.

Her shot was true. The Thirty Pointer shuddered and then grew still as the shock of the bullet exploding its heart rent through its body as it died.

And then the darkness was still besides Lily's heavy breathing and the ringing in her ears.

She crept towards the still creature, raising the butt to her shoulder but keeping the barrel and the light aimed in the general direction of the deer. When she came within feet of it, she found massive amounts of blood pooling beneath it. She wasted no time in finding a stick and prodding it in the eye. It did not blink, and only then did she truly believe that the huge deer was dead.

She set the rifle down and unfastened the flashlight. In a haze, she knelt next to it and began to count the points to see what she could determine as the official count on the symmetrical, typical rack. Sure enough, it was more than thirty – the most careful counters had come up with 32 from Lenny's picture. Lily found 34.

She knelt like that for a while, in awe of the animal in front of her, almost feeling like she had, in fact, taken it in the course of a hunt. But she knew she hadn't. She knew she had just delivered mercy. It was an accident that killed it – a freak, absurd twist in the saga – an abrupt, inglorious end to the legendary beast that had danced through the dreams of an entire region of buck-fevered hunters.

If she had killed it in the course of a hunt, she would have begun to field dress the animal, removing its guts and putting it in the bed of her truck to take into town and register before hanging it up back in Mr. Leonardson's garage. But now she wasn't sure what the best thing to do was. This was roadkill. Perhaps it was best to call the DNR and have them send a warden. They'd take care of it, or they'd tell her what to do with it. She couldn't just leave it – people had to know what happened. They needed to know that it was over.

Just then, she heard a car coming down the road the same way that she had come, and then headlights came into view. She hoped the driver would just carry on past her, but that seemed unlikely. To her dismay, the vehicle slowed and pulled over to the side of the road, coming to rest just a few yards from where she was kneeling by the deer. She stood up and squinted into the lights, trying to see who it was.

The driver got out of the truck and left it running. It was a man wearing a hat and bundled up for winter weather. His silhouette advanced towards her.

"Hello?" said Lily.

Then her heart dropped. Emerging from the glare of the headlights was the man from the field – the man who had been wandering in Mr. Leonardson's property the summer before.

He walked up to her and stopped.

"Well, it's the Girl Scout. Whatcha got there, Girl Scout…" his voice trailed away as he looked towards the deer and realized what it was. "Jesus Christ," he whispered.

Lily was afraid, and she wished she was holding the rifle instead of the flashlight.

"I hit it with my car," she said.

The man's eyes were wide as he stared at the animal and slowly shook his head.

"Do…do you know what I should do with it? I thought I'd call the DNR."

Then the man looked towards her rifle and his eyes narrowed. He gestured towards the weapon.

"Whatcha got that for then? Say you hit it with your car ah? Sure you're not out doing some shining?"

"No, no I was on the way home and it ran out in front of me. But I shot it after to put it out of its misery."

"Sure yah did."

"I did."

The man stood there, nodding. Lily could only just make out his face, but she thought she could see an idea or realization spring to life, and then his features set into stony resolve. He turned and walked back to his truck without a word. He got in and pulled out in the road, but went into an immediate U-turn, and then began to back the truck up towards her, parking it almost on top of the deer. He got out and walked towards her again.

"Wh-what are you doing?"

He didn't answer. He lowered the tailgate of his truck and climbed in. Then Lily realized that he had a pulley system, and she gasped. Working quickly and wordlessly, the man grabbed the end of the chain and pulled it forward, and in moments he had it wrapped around the deer's torso.

"You're taking it?"

He still didn't answer. He went back to the bed of the truck and began to turn a crank, and the deer was lifted off the ground towards the bed of the truck, blood flowing from its wound. The realization hit Lily with a thud.

"You can't take that deer! You didn't shoot it, but you're going to say that you did! Stop!"

The man didn't say anything but shot her a withering glance.

"You can't do this – it isn't right!"

Her pleas for decency were falling on deaf ears. Fighting back panic, she turned to logic.

"People will know you didn't kill it. Its legs are broken. Or its back."

The deer was almost into the bed of the truck. The man stopped turning the crank for a moment.

"Can you tell its legs are broken? See a broken spine?"

Lily didn't answer. She had to admit that she couldn't.

"I didn't think so."

He went back to turning the crank.

"There's the damage on my truck."

"People hit deer all the time."

"The ballistics."

The deer was in the truck, and the man went to the tailgate and closed it. He paused. Then he walked towards her again but stopped amidst the pool of blood and squatted. He started feeling about in the grass, and then he reached into the dirt and pulled out a bloody bullet. He held it up to her and smiled.

"I wouldn't have thought of that. Thanks."

He stood up and turned away from her, heading back to his truck.

Lily picked up her rifle and suddenly the idea was on her that she could kill him, that she wanted to. It would be easy. The desire flared up in her and then was gone in an instant.

"I'll tell," she yelled after him.

He stopped and turned back towards her. He didn't even react to the sight of her holding the gun.

"Fuck you," he said. And then he got into his truck and left, the antlers of the Thirty Pointer just visible in the bed of his truck as he sped away.

Lily's shoulders heaved and she sank to her knees, emitting a shuddering sob. She cried for a good while, panic and adrenaline rushing over her. She was just getting her composure again when headlights came into view. Again she hoped they would speed on by, but again they slowed and pulled over, and again she shielded her eyes to see what she could see.

This time the driver got out of the vehicle quickly.

"Lily!"

It was Leif, running towards her.

"Leif!"

He ran up to her and stopped, confusion on his face at the sight of her and the rifle and the blood on the ground.

"What happened? Are you okay?" He knelt beside her and put his hand on her shoulder.

Lily began sobbing again. "I killed the Thirty Pointer, Leif. I killed it."

"You what? Where? Where is it? Why are you crying?"

She fought through the sobs and told him what had happened.

"And then he just left. He left and then you got here. You probably passed him on the way here."

Leif's face was pale and his eyes were concerned. Lily hoped that he would know what to do, that he would jump into action, but she didn't know what that action was.

He didn't jump up and chase after the man. Instead, he wrapped his arm around her shoulders and allowed her to bury her head in his shoulder and cry.

"You're okay, Lily. You're safe. You're safe. You did the right thing. We're going to go to your grandparents. And if you want, we'll call Jan. Okay?"

"Okay." She sniffed. "It's just not fair. It's just not fair. It's not supposed to be like this. It's not right."

"No, it isn't." He sighed. "Maybe it never was."

Twenty-Five: A Late Hour

Leif followed Lily to her home and parked behind her in the driveway. Lily went to the back seat to get her stuff and Leif hurried up to help her.

"I can get it," she said.

"I know you can, but I'll help if it's okay."

Lily didn't say anything but let him take the rifle in its case.

They walked together up to the house. The night was getting cold and the wind had picked up. The automatic light on the porch turned on as they approached. Lily knew the door would be locked and her hands were full so she rang the doorbell rather than getting a key.

"Lily…"

She turned to look up at him, her eyes sad.

"I called Jan on the way here."

She gave little reaction. "I sort of thought you might."

"Are you upset?"

She shrugged. "I've kind of given up having control over things."

Leif winced. "It feels like that sometimes. But you always have the ability to…"

The door opened and Lily's grandparents appeared behind the screen door, which her grandfather quickly opened, like he could tell something was not quite right.

"Lily, come in." Then he looked up at Leif.

"Grandpa, Grandma, this is Leif. He's…a friend of a friend."

The old man gave Leif a suspicious look but stood aside to let him in.

"But why is here? And why does he have your rifle?"

"I'll tell you," said Lily. "But can we come inside and get warm first?"

Now the old woman also appeared to know something was not right, and she nodded without prodding any further.

Soon the four of them were seated around the kitchen table with pho and hot chocolate. Leif was surprised but pleased by the combination.

They sat in silence, eating and sipping. The three adults were all waiting on Lily. She quickly ate, and then she was ready to talk. This time, as she related the events of the evening, she did not cry. Rather, she was stone faced and sullen. Her grandparents looked on with worried expressions. Leif watched them, trying to get the measure of them.

When she was finished telling the story, her grandmother made worried noises and her grandfather growled.

"A typical American boy. A goddamn little shit," he said.

Lily and Leif exchanged a brief look. The old man appeared to not know or care if he had given offense.

"This is why you should not hunt," said the grandmother.

"The Americans ruin it. She tries to do something good. Be responsible. And this man walked over her. Trampled her. Told her what to do. Damn him. That little shit."

The man's gaze was ice, his jaw stone, and his fists iron. Leif was glad the old man never met his father all those years ago.

Lily had nothing more to say.

Then the doorbell rang. Only then did Lily's face change into one of nervous anticipation.

"I'll get it," said Leif, nearly falling over as he rushed to get out of his chair. He went towards the door without waiting for the homeowners to respond.

He opened the door to find Jan waiting on the porch. He stepped outside and let the door close behind him.

"You're here," said Leif.

"I am. You didn't think I would?"

"I didn't know. I know this is…"

"Insane?"

Leif nodded.

"But maybe this needed to happen eventually," said Jan. "And maybe this is the kind of time to do it. What were the odds you'd be the first one to find her? Maybe this is supposed to happen."

"Do you believe things are *supposed* to happen?"

Jan smiled. "I don't know. But sometimes it just really seems like it, doesn't it?"

"Yes. Yes it does."

"I know that I'm *supposed* to clean my gutters. And I know it's kind of challenging for me to do it because I'm small. How…cosmically ordained that a big strong man…who is also funny, and kind, albeit lazy and a bit of a fool, happens to live next door, and happens to have a very open schedule?"

Leif grinned.

"So it would seem."

They hugged.

"Let's go, Leif. Whatever happens next, things will be different, and, for better and worse, none of it will be easy."

They went into the house to find that Lily and her grandparents had made their way into the entryway. The old couple had stern expressions. Lily stepped away from them and moved closer to her aunt.

"Grandma, Grandpa, I think there's another story to tell."

Before anyone else could say anything, Jan reached into her coat pocket and drew out a photograph. She held it out to her parents, who looked at each other and then stepped forward to take it.

Her mother covered her mouth with her hand as she gasped. Her father was already blinking back tears. Jan was holding her breath. Lily looked on, confused. Somehow, Leif already knew what it was.

It was a photo of a much younger Jan, posing for a group photo with her parents, Khoi, Pham, and baby Lily.

The secret ingredient.

Epilogue: Winter Back from War

As soon as he stepped outside, Leif regretted shaving his beard. The cold air and the driving wind scoured his face and neck and took his breath away. He cursed and buried his chin in his scarf and pulled his knit cap down to cover more of his forehead. Then he wasted no time trudging through the snow to his truck. He would be sure to shovel the walkway when he got back, but it made no sense now as it was still snowing. It was convenient for him to live with his parents until he bought a home, but having to park outside the garage all winter was less than ideal.

When he turned the key in the ignition, the engine revved and then sputtered out. He tried a second time with no luck. He paused and took a deep breath and hoped for the best. He turned the key again, and this time the engine roared into life.

He backed down the driveway and then drove the familiar route towards downtown Badger Creek. In high school, he would have gunned it down this first road, but he was in no hurry and the conditions were less than ideal.

The streets were quiet. It was the middle of the day and tourist season was a distant memory, and most people wouldn't be out unless they had to be. Leif felt the need to be out, even if it couldn't quite be called a necessity.

House after house, block after block, the town was all the same. Nothing had changed so far as he could tell since the day his mother and father drove him to the airport in Milwaukee where he would get on a plane bound for Parris Island by way of Savannah. He drove past the same Christmas decorations in parks and on lampposts. He drove past the same businesses and restaurants (except for the diner on the corner of 14th and Madison, which for some reason could never support a restaurant longer than a year or two). The few people he did see looked familiar, even if he didn't know their names. It even seemed like the same sky and trees. The same cold air.

There was something reassuring in the sameness. But there was something disappointing, too.

He pulled up in front of Sully's Café. There were only a couple of other vehicles parked there. The sight of the familiar homemade sign swinging above the door stirred a craving in him – though that might have also been an itch to take a quick cigarette. It was too cold for that, and he was too hungry, so he got out of the car in a slight hurry and strode to the door, crunching salt pellets beneath his heavy boots.

A bell jingled as he stepped into the small café. He stomped snow off his boots and shivered.

At the sound of the bell, Sully himself, who was at the kitchen window, looked up and recognized him immediately.

"Leif!"

"Hi, Mr. Sullivan."

"Oh just call me Sully. You're a man grown!" Sully came out of the kitchen, leaving the sizzle of the grill and fryers in the hands of whomever else was back there – if there was anyone else back there. "And you *have* grown. Not just up, but…you're a strapping young man there guy." Sully was beaming, as only someone who has seen someone grow up before them can.

"Ah it's just the heavy coat," said Leif, even though he knew he had put on a lot of muscle since enlisting.

"You back now? For good?"

Leif nodded.

"Well I'm honored to feast the returning hero. It's on the house today."

"Oh, you don't have to-…"

"No course I don't! But I want to," said Sully, putting his hand on Leif's shoulder. "Kim, come show Leif to a clean table, and give him nothing but the very best service."

A middle-aged woman emerged from the dining room, smiling.

"Oh Sully, I give nothing but the best to all our guests."

"Course you do, but now I want your best to be even better for our patriotic patron."

Leif blushed, adding color to his already flushed face.

"As you say boss. Right this way, sir! Good to see you, by the way."

Leif was about to follow, but first turned to acknowledge the restaurateur.

"Thanks, Sully."

"Of course. Oh, hey, can I go ahead and get it started? The usual?"

Leif hesitated just a moment. He had been thinking about this Sullyburger since he got on the troop transport in Bagram. But there was an entire menu of food that he was sure was just as good. In a world of the same, maybe it was worth trying something new. He had heard good things about the fried perch sandwich and the

Reuben.

But he hadn't come here for something different. He had come here for something familiar.

"Oh yah," said Leif. "The usual."

Outside, the snow continued to fall, much as it had the winter before, much as it would the winter after, swirling gusts of a million crystals, all of them unique.

ACKNOWLEDGEMENTS

Many people contributed to the process of writing and editing this book with nothing more than gratitude in return. Thank you to everyone who read this ahead of its release. Thank you to my writing group, D-Mac's Dorks, for the ongoing community of feedback and encouragement. Thank you, Lauren and Khoi, for making sure this white guy portrayed the Vietnamese American experience with respect and some measure of accuracy. Thank you, God, for being very good to this very bad Christian.

ABOUT THE AUTHOR

Peter Dahl

This is Peter Dahl's first published novel. He blogs from time to time at eloquentmumbler.com. He has a Master's Degree in English from Oregon State University. He grew up in northeast Wisconsin and now lives in southwest Wisconsin with his cat, Hei Bai.